Gossip Girl Fanfic Novella

Gossip Girl Fanfic Novella

Charlie Markbreiter

Illustrations by River Lorelei Ramirez

Chicago: Kenning Editions, 2022

For Kato Trieu and Lauren Berlant

"Would a nose job make me look better in a blazer
Would a car fire be faster than a hair removal laser
Is a pet cat gluten-free
Would I still be sad if I was five foot three
Should I sing real fast
Should I fuck my dad
Should I marry Darren Aronofsky"

—Macy Rodman, "The Aronofsky Method/Huge If True" (2021)

GOSSIP GIRL CAST:

Nate

The beautiful himbo. Bernie Madoff is his dad. Nate's main vibe is empty. His main mood is happy but sad.

Dan

Vengeful. Resentful. Alt nerd. Lives in a gorgeous Williamsburg loft, but, because it's 2007, everyone thinks he's poor. Does he love Serena? Or does he just love to wear vests?

Serena

Popular. It Girl. If you haven't met her, you have. In a baby doll dress. Boho blazer rumpled look. Serena isn't mean, though. For the most part, she wants to be on your side. Except when she can't help herself.

Blair

"The Queen" loves headbands. *Breakfast at Tiffany's*. Her best friend is Serena; Serena is her number one enemy. She's in love with Chuck, her number one enemy. Her mom neglects her. Her gay dad lives in France.

Chuck

Every show needs a villain. If the devil can talk, can he kiss? Chuck's mother died giving birth to him; his father is Jeff Bezos. Every love story is Oedipal; that's why it's love.

Jenny

Jenny always knew that she had a supporting role. She was Dan's little sister. Would she ever be anything more? American Apparel-core, Urban Outfitter-core.

Vanessa

The moral conscience. The artist. Dan's best Brooklyn friend. How did I get here. How do I get out.

Rufus

Dan and Jenny have a sexy dad. Former rock star turned Williamsburg gallerist. The kind of plot that makes sense on TV. So of course he has a crush on Serena's mom.

Lily

The facelift's eternal return on your investment is Lily's skin. Wrinkle free, just like a Tesla. Serena's mom.

Gossip Girl: the Blog

Who writes the omniscient narrator, who says what you wish you could say? You hate that you love me. I mean that.

gossip girl
welcome
gossip
pics
parties
links

Preface

"Hey, Upper East Siders. Gossip Girl here. And I have the biggest news ever."

Almost every episode of *Gossip Girl* begins like this. We're Upper East Siders; *Gossip Girl* tells us we are. But also, we aren't. We never will be. All we can do is look inside.

The original show—which aired on the CW, America's favorite teen drama network—started in 2007, hitting the tail end of the Bush era, swerving through the Financial Crash, and ending in 2012, midway through the Obama years.

And yet the YA books that the series is based on begin much earlier (2002-2011), making them a time capsule of the aughts, back when history had supposedly ended and there was nothing left but the diagonal horizon of progress, and tying up loose ends.

Gossip Girl follows *Gossip Girl*, an anonymous blog, and the prep school students she reports on, who snitch on each other for likes.

In 2006 (inspired by *Gossip Girl*?), the media blog *Gawker* combined its weekly celeb sighting column with a live Google Map of New York, allowing fans to track their favorite celebrities in real time. They called it the *Gawker* Stalker. By 2010, the site was regularly posting shots of the *Gossip Girl* cast: Chuck, in a beanie, white v-neck and aviators, walking on set with a bag of take-out; Serena (Blake Lively) and Dan (Penn Badgely), then a real-life couple, dining at a New American eatery.

Part One

S1E3: "Poison Ivy"
Nate's POV

Once Nate's dad was busted for being Bernie Madoff, each member of the Archibald family retreated from the public eye in their own special way. Mrs. Archibald holed up in their Hamptons place, tending the garden. Mr. Archibald, also known as "The Captain," fled to his true love–his offshore accounts–setting up a new luxurious life in an unnamed Caribbean freeport.

Nate was already private, but scandal made it worse. He didn't want to ask for help, didn't even want to tell Chuck, his best friend, that they were totally broke. When the FBI seized the assets (including furniture) in the Archibald's Upper East Side apartment, Nate lived there anyway, sleeping on the wooden floor of his hollowed out former life.

Did he really have to punish himself like that? Couldn't someone have borrowed an air mattress for our martyr king?

Of course, there were other reasons for craving austerity and secrecy. If procuring puberty blockers now is hard (they're currently trying to ban them for kids in the UK and parts of the US), getting blockers in 1998 was impossible, not because the chemicals didn't exist (they had for decades), but because trans people didn't exist yet, at least not in the public eye. The Archibalds weren't pro-trans. They still aren't. It's just that child Nate kept trying to hang herself from her canopy bed or throw herself down the spiral marble stairs, and when the Captain uscrewed the bedroom door, took away the boy toys, and said, "If you kill yourself, I'll kill you," Nate said nothing, just waited til he left, opened the front door, and walked into Park Avenue traffic, at which point, Mrs. Archibald figured she'd rather have a son than a suicidal toddler. *And if she killed herself? Can you imagine? What they'd say? About our family? You and me?*

Luckily, the Captain's two talents were being rich and being a bully. They bribed the family doctor, who got blockers from NYU Langone hospital and made the testosterone himself, purchasing the yams wholesale from another Upper East Side aristobrat family's Marie Antoinette-style farm. Nate left his kindergarten year at Constance Billard halfway through, moving to the Hamptons for a year, where he was homeschooled by a fleet of tutors, Medici-style. When Nate came back, he was a boy. The Archibalds enrolled him at St Jude's.

If you knew him as a girl, no you didn't.

S2E12: "It's a Wonderful Lie"

Cory Kennedy was the first Internet It Girl. Her fame, according to actress and Cory Kennedy scholar Ruby McCollister, lasted from 2005 to 2009, just after the 2008 financial crash. For McCollister, Kennedy marks the shift between the early-aughts era star machine (built around tabloids, paparazzi, scandal, and national if not global stardom) and the Web 2.0 epoch, in which stars are niche and made by the internet.

The "paparazzi gold rush era" was ostensibly born in 2002, which is when "Stars: They're Just Like Us" debuted in *US Weekly* magazine. The column featured celebs doing random shit: picking up a FedEx delivery in sweatpants, drinking a venti Starbucks iced coffee, jogging. People lost their minds. A *Slate* article argued that reading "Stars: They're Just Like Us" was like watching an extraterrestrial pump gas. The actors had exited the movie. Now they were pumping gas.

The column's founding moment is equally draped in self-mythology. According to legend (the internet), "Stars" began with Bonnie Fuller, a new features editor brought in to jump start lagging sales. Parsing paparazzi photos wired in from the night before, Fuller flipped past glossy, staged nights of singularity–vacations, parties, movie premiers–before zeroing in on a photo of Drew Barrymore bending down to grab a coin from the sidewalk. "Look at Drew Barrymore picking up a penny," she said. "It's like, stars, they're just like us." During the paparazzi gold rush era, a pic of a star being just like us went, on average, for $5-15k a pop.

In Kennedy's online debut, posted around the anniversary of JFK's death, she is fifteen and wearing a yellow Lacoste dress, black converse, and leg warmers; the caption reads "CORY KENNEDY JFK." McCollister argues that every It Girl is both a symbol of her time and a harbinger of things to come (doom). An LA party photographer–the twenty-year-old Mark Hunter, who fifteen-year-old Kennedy will soon date–posts the image on his website, which is named after his professional alias: the Cobrasnake.

The phrase "go viral" didn't really exist in 2005. Virality, what Wikipedia defines as "the capacity to attract an enormous audience on a user-friendly platform," didn't fully start until YouTube took off. The rise of online virality as a genre–exemplified by YouTube clips like "Numa Numa" (2006), "Shoes" (2006, weird gender vibes) and "Charlie Bit My Finger" (2007, my name is Charlie)–coincided with the rise of the viral celebrity. Today, we might say that the first Cobrasnake image of JFK Cory Kennedy went viral. Indie sleaze first time around.

If Kennedy was the proto-Instagram It Girl, then, McCollister argues, fashion and party blogs like The Cobrasnake were proto-Instagram. It's where you would go to be seen online. The Cobrasnake started noticing that whenever he posted a photo of Cory, his website traffic would skyrocket. And it wasn't just the numbers; it was about who was looking (fashion people). He remembers thinking (and then telling a *Los Angeles Times* interviewer), "I'm not a superstar. But if I can create a superstar, it'll be good for my career, for her career, for all of us." There was no algorithm, dictating whose content would appear at the top of your feed. Just the Cobrasnake rawdogging it, calculating which pics of his fifteen year old muse/girlfriend he could most easily monetize.

Around 2012, McCollister notes that everyone on Instagram started to seem like they were selling something. "And it's because they were." What happened? "I mean, the Recession happened," McCollister says. Suddenly, no one could afford to keep doing this shit for free, building a stockpile of clout that could hopefully tide you from gig to party, party back to gig. You needed an alternate revenue stream, one that would generate real cash. If there's cultural nostalgia for the Cobrasnake/Cory Kennedy era, perhaps what we feel is longing for a less commodified online. As social media becomes more extractive, we manufacture nostalgia for pre-Instagram times.

In an interview with *i-D Vice*, "Tik Tok DIY musician" pinkpanthress was asked why her work "revolved around samples from the 90s and early 00s." She responded by saying, "The music was so unpolished and cool...I feel like people weren't afraid of being a little bit cringe. It was all way more experimental." Life was more like a finsta or a photo dump, less varnished and buffed. The music video for pinkpanthress's recent hit "Just For Me" looks like an iPod: middle school dance vibes, post-scene, emo-core. Chunky laptop flip-phone-core.

The vibe is school dance dream pop and yet the inspo is horror, death. In the same interview, pinkpanthress says that her main visual reference points are "horror films. I love them all, especially *Saw*. And emo music videos from Linkin Park and Papa Roach." Necropolitical new nostalgic. She mostly goes by pinkpanthress. It's almost impossible to find her real name online.

Eventually, even the Cobrasnake blog caved, died, and was reborn as "The Cobrasnake" shop, which sells vintage deadstock and "festival wear," a band shirt priced at $500, things like that. You could argue that Cory wasn't selling anything, at least not at first, and that this was her magic. She wasn't trying to be an artist, a writer, an influencer, or a fashion designer. She was just being herself and having fun and getting paid for it. As everyone should be. Though, of course, she was also selling something: her it-girl image, herself. She had to. It's what everyone wanted from her.

As Biz Sherbert argues in "Millennialcore: the It-Girl Industrial Complex," Cory's look–"the waifish glitter-and-grunge"–feels prescient. Cory's dirty hipster vibe was an antidote to "the shimmering early-2000s bimbo (who was hyperfeminine and smelled like the mall and vanilla)." The media empire which had produced her had just been gutted, plus showing off your wealth felt tacky now. As Sherbert notes, this shift towards visual austerity was reflected in high fashion. "Prada, Dries Van Noten, and Lanvin all sent subdued collections down the runway to match the sober and sparing spirit of the recession." The exception to this was Marc Jacobs, whose eighties club-core collection felt like a "'down-and-out but let's get high' response to hard times." Cobrasnake pictures don't give I processed my trauma vibes. They give I was hit on the head with a brick and kept going.

If there's a Cory Kennedy stand-in on *Gossip Girl*, it's Jenny, of course: the fucked-up bangs, the eyeliner, the being underage and hooking up with adults, the glamor, the sadness. How do you process history?

S2E3: Elevator
Serena's POV

Dan always has to be right. It's the only thing he has. Citywide blackout, Dan and Serena trapped in an elevator. Five years after invading Iraq. Bear Stearns has just tanked.

When Dan calls, a doorman says they'll just have to wait until the power comes back on.

"You should have mentioned my name," Serena says.

"You always think you're special."

"I just live in the building, Dan." *When she's right and he's wrong, she just has to put up with it, has to make it seem like it was his idea.* "If you're not going to call again, then let's not talk about it anymore." Serena loves chaos, you just don't notice at first because she's so nice. But when she isn't chaotic, she's practical: the elevator doesn't have AC.

To spite her and himself, Dan calls again. When he mentions Serena, the doorman, embarrassed, promises to send someone up ASAP.

"What do you want, Dan? For me to never say my name?" Instead of just admitting that he's wrong, Dan tries to escape. He jumps and knocks a tile in the ceiling, which flips up like a trap door.

"I just don't think it's fair."

"You know what? Life's not fair. Because it doesn't fit with the way you, Dan Humphrey, think things should be. But why are you always right?" In this case, he is right. Things should be different. But what does that even change?

Dan propels himself up through the ceiling and falls on the floor with a snapping sound that makes Serena wince.

An instrumental interlude plays.

S2E10: "Bonfire of the Vanity"

Gordon's POV

It was hot and Gordon didn't have AC. He made watermelon salad for dinner, dragging his box fan into the living room and plugging it next to the table as they ate. Later, unable to sleep, he would grab the ice pack he'd used to soothe a running injury and put it on his face.

Since the reboot was coming out and since he'd worked on the original fifteen years ago and hadn't done much since, he and his roommate, Rio, had decided to binge all seven seasons of *Gossip Girl*.

"It used to be on Netflix for free but I guess they moved it to HBO," said Rio, as she did lines of K. Luckily, their other roommate, Effie, a brand consultant, had an HBO account. "Okay. Here we go."

"Where do you want to start?"

"Let's do one of the episodes you worked on."

"Come on."

"What? That's literally the point."

"The point is–"

"Didn't you do this one?"

In the episode, Dan, attempting to copycat his sister's callous ambition, pretends to be friends with Chuck so that he can write about the Bass's for *New York Magazine*. He finagles a fake internship with Chuck's dad, who is Jeff Bezos-coded.

"God. This show is just one long unpaid internship." The door opens and shuts quietly as Effie walks into the living room, home late from work.

"Do you want to watch with us?"

"No, but thank you. Too hot." Effie takes off her gladiator sandals and slips into her bedroom, which has AC. In the world of *Gossip Girl*, things are happening. Things always are. The show feels so that we don't have to. Feelings just happen and we get to watch, just like life.

S1E9: "Blair Waldorf Must Pie!"
Nate's POV

For Serena's seventh birthday, the van der Woodsen's rented out the carousel in Central Park and half the Big Apple Circus, so you could watch a magic show or get a balloon animal while you waited to ride. Nate got on the carousel and felt nausea almost immediately.

"I think I want to get off," he said, and closed his eyes. Serena held his hand.

"It'll be okay."

Later, Blair, unable to contain her jealousy, unable to express the need for love as anything other than spite, beelined to Nate, staggering out of the carousel, and said, "Remember when you were a girl?" Nate felt his brain split off from his body. He was a brain in a jar with the brain water splashing out.

"Nate was never a girl," he heard Blair's faggot father say. "You're imagining that, my dear."

"If Nate wasn't a girl then how come he used to go to Constance Billard with me? Constance Billard is a *girl school*." Mr. Waldorf smiled at the other parents.

"Blair has such a rich imagination." He embraced his daughter, picking her up and holding her in his arms. He was wearing a button down and an argyle v-neck sweater despite the heat.

Even after Mr. Waldorf left his family, abandoning his family and moving to France with his gay lover, Blair still insisted that her father was the better parent, that he was the only one who really knew her, loved her, cared.

Nate watched them walk off. Nate watched himself vomit next to a nearby spruce.

Histories of the Transgender Child by Jules Gill-Peterson

Trans kids are typically cast as a twenty-first century invention, not just by mainstream eugenics-lite publications like the *New York Times*, but by tenured trans studies scholars. This is a lie. As Jules Gill-Peterson proves in *Histories of the Transgender Child* (2018), trans kids predate the medical industrial complex; there have been trans kids as long as there have been kids. But the very definition of transsexuality–and of the gender binary itself–was conceived and codified alongside experiments done on trans childrens' bodies, and carried out by clinicians who maintained a stake in their own preconceived, hegemonic notions of sex and gender.

These experiments, which mostly took place at Johns Hopkins hospital, were mediated by race and class, as is everything. When it came to white children, Gill-Peterson argues that the capacity to alter gender via hormone treatments and surgery was seen as a marker of "plasticity," a positive moniker for potentiality and change that could easily be mapped onto a Cold War American nationalism that prided itself on scientific "progress"and whiteness itself. "Sex and gender were reconceived as plastic phenotypes during the twentieth century," Gill-Peterson writes, "which makes all human embodiment, including cisgender forms, a racial formation." White trans children were abstracted into metaphors. On the other hand, clinicians interpreted Black kids' dysphoria through pre-existing racist rhetorics of deviance and criminality, and turned it into a justification for present and future punishment. Their dysphoria was often misdiagnosed as schizophrenia.

The racialization of transness as a diagnostic category was a gatekeeping effect, determining who was able to access already sparse surgeries and hormone replacement therapy. As Gill-Peterson writes, "Because the concept of plasticity was abstractly racialized by medical science as a synonym for whiteness, in the clinic, it had real demographic effects. The overwhelming majority of trans patients seen at institutions of medicine were white." The trans child was implicitly racialized as white so that white children could access medical transition most easily.

S2E13: "O Brother, Where Bart Thou?"
Chuck's POV

Chuck takes the Oedipus myth too literally and accidentally kills his father. Since he can't touch his father's dead body, he looks for the private investigator files that his father kept in his office. Bart kept files on everybody. Unable, in the last instance, to fully bear it, Chuck blames Lily instead. It's complicated.

Lily looks good. She's giving, *I transitioned later, but I'm fish*. She's giving, *I'm rich but also I'm a good person and I can afford the face peels that keep you thirty-eight forever*. She's happy that Bart is dead. She loves Rufus. Chuck can sense it. Whatever is making Lily happy, he wants it dead.

Perhaps it's worth recapping the episode for clarity. Halfway through, Chuck sees Lily flirting with Rufus at the Snowflake Ball. Everything important must be seasonal. In another narrative strand, Jenny tricks Vanessa, giving her a dress to wear without telling her that it's see-through.

She and Vanessa are meant to be sisters.

At the gala's narrative climax, a spotlight hits Vanessa, *Carrie*-style. Anyone with a body can be naked. That's the problem with it. Six years later, Rihanna would accept a CFDA Fashion Icon Award in a body con shimmer gown, fully transparent except for 200,000 Swarovski crystals and a pink stole.

Chuck, playing the Good Son at last, the most Loyal Boy, calls his father and tells him to come to the Snowflake Ball. Something is happening. Something Bad. As Bart's limo shoots over–to do what? It doesn't matter. He's hit by a car and killed.

When Chuck confronts Lily, it's unclear what the writers were going for. Chuck could be Tony Soprano but also he could be Hamlet; it's not clear, but it doesn't have to be. All that matters is that something deep, something Intense and Literary, is being indexed here.

"I can't look at you, Lily," says Chuck, "because you disgust me. Betraying my father with Rufus Humphrey."

"I did *no* such thing."

"He was coming to fight for you. Talk about dying for nothing."

If Chuck were to keep taking the Oedipal triangle literally, then he'd sleep with Lily, not kill her. Instead, he runs down contemporary art coated stairs, as if he'd misplaced the script.

My Fave Puberty

The *Gossip Girl* cast are meant to be teens, but everyone looks early twenties. When *Gossip Girl* first aired in 2007, Blair (Leighton Meester) was twenty-one; Nate (Chace Crawford) was twenty-two. When Crawford was an actual teen, he modeled for Abercrombie and Hollister, one of those guys who stands outside the store, shirtless, showing off their abs at the mall. It was totally fine and normal for passersby to take pictures with the Abercrombie/Hollister models and not pay them, the way you take pictures with Goofy and Mickey at Disney World.

This second adolescence, going through puberty again in your twenties, in front of everyone–there is, one might say, something very transgender about that.

S2E10: Writing
Dan's POV

Unlike Hannah Horvath or Carrie Bradshaw, Dan is a really bad writer, despite the fact that his character archetype is "sensitive nerd." Dan somehow fails to write anything for his summer writing internship, fails to procure a letter of recommendation. It's unclear if the internship was paid.

Back at St. Jude's for fall term and the start of Season 2, Dan is assigned another writer/mentor figure, a Hemingway-type who tells him his work is boring. Dan is essentially doing auto-fiction at this point, though it isn't called that. Dan says, "I just tried to write what I know."

"Well, what you know is boring." The writer/mentor encourages Dan to exploit people and use them as material.

"Never. That's unethical." In truth, of course, Dan is already doing it. He's *Gossip Girl*.

S1E5: "Hope Sinks"
Gordon's POV

Marcus said if I didn't do it, I was an idiot. "We all know you need the money."

"I'm doing fine."

"I mean sure. You're doing fine. But–and I'm not saying this to be an asshole, I'm saying this because you're a thirty-four year old man…"

"Alright…"

"And we love you."

"I know."

"We do."

"I know that."

"But whenever we go out to dinner, which we do at least once a week...I'm just saying."

"What."

"I don't know. I always pay." *I couldn't look at him.* "I'm not trying to shame you."

"I never ask you to pay."

"I know."

"You always offer."

"It's not that I even mind. I just…" He paused. Lit a cigarette. "I just think it would be good for you. You wouldn't even have to tell anyone. It's not a lead writer credit, don't flatter yourself."

"It's not even *Gossip Girl 2*. It's *Gossip Girl 3*."

"It's 50k. What even is your problem?"

The waiter came by and cleared our plates.

"How was everything?"

"So good. Thanks."

"Do you guys want to see a dessert menu?"

"I'm okay–"

"Yes," Marcus said. "We would. And espresso for me."

"Wow. Coffee at night. That's Euro."

"It's for digestion. Well. And I'm also going out after this."

"Oh nice. What are you going to do?"

"Just some work thing. But then Brbbbbb is doing a set at Flower Hole."

The waiter came by with the espresso and our dessert menus. Marcus asked him for a little steamed milk. The waiter came back with steamed milk in a porcelain cup with a fluted spout.

"Wow. That's such a good idea."

"What?"

"For the coffee."

"Oh." Marcus laughed. "I learned about this when I worked as a barista. Cortados." He mixed the steamed milk with his coffee, stirred in a sugar cube, finished the scalding drink in a sip. "Anyway. Just tell me. What's your fear."

"Of writing for *Gossip Girl 3*? I mean–it's not even fear. Just like... I don't know. People already don't take me seriously."

"Serious? What do you want to be serious for?"

"'Serious' isn't the word because I know being serious isn't cool. Like, writing isn't cool..."

"Being a writer is cool."

"Being a writer is glam. *Writing* is uncool. It always has been. Nerd shit. You know I'm right." Marcus shut his eyes and massaged his forehead as if he had a headache, or a third eye awakening painfully.

"God. Why do I always have to tell you what to do." We'd met in college. I'd done well, was seen as being witty or some Harry Potter shit like that. Our friend group had always clowned Marcus for being the dumb "film and Econ" bro. The waiter passed Marcus the check. He tipped twenty percent. He always did. As we left the restaurant, he said he'd text me after his work thing.

"Yes, for sure, thank you." Both of us knowing I wouldn't show. We hugged like brothers.

S2E12: "It's a Wonderful Lie"
Nate's POV

The Captain liked being as naked as possible. In summer especially. Guests would come and he'd greet them shirtless, in a bathing suit, in tennis shorts and an open button down, ridges of the only slightly sagging six pack visible underneath tanned and curling stomach hair. When Nate's parents had met at Yale, the Captain was the captain of the varsity swim team. That's where the nickname was from.

"It's because your dad asked people to call him that," Nate's mom had told him once when she was drunk, which she often was. "That's how it began." Sometimes the rumors you start about yourself are the only ones that stick.

When it was just them at home, the Captain would often walk around fully naked–to show off? To prove that this was his home? Nate stared at his father's dick with repulsion and jealousy.

As soon as Nate could walk, the Captain signed him up for swimming lessons, then for a swim team, but it was no use. Nate couldn't figure out how to kick.

"Move your legs!" his dad would scream, bending down poolside during races to make sure Nate could hear. Chlorine flooded Nate's mouth.

"If you're going to be a boy, you have to be good at sports." Sitting in their limo. Nate's lips still blue from the pool. "Otherwise, what's the point. Go back to being a girl."

"Maybe he just doesn't like swimming," said Mrs. Archibald. "He doesn't have to do it just because you did."

"What's wrong with swimming?"

"Nothing," murmured Nate's mom, and later, when they were back at the apartment, she asked Nate if he wanted to quit the swim team, and he said yes and started to cry.

"You should do lacrosse," Chuck told him later at school. "The girls love lacrosse players. Trust me." Nate wasn't sure how Chuck knew this. Chuck didn't play lacrosse. He didn't play any sports. They were ten. But he trusted Chuck without thinking because it was easier than having to think for himself.

"Okay," he said. "I'll do it. What's lacrosse."

If swimming was like being a girl, where everything was difficult and he didn't know the rules, lacrosse was like being a boy in that it came to him easily. This despite the awkwardness of the sport itself: the big stick with its weird little basket, the heavy ball made of vulcanized rubber. Nate started carrying a lacrosse stick around even when he wasn't going to or from practice and games. It made him feel like he had a prop.

Once Nate became a lacrosse star–captain of his middle school team, then recruited to a city-wide travel league–Nate thought the Captain would be happy. Instead, he seemed to resent his son's success. If he showed up to games, he was critical after. *He doesn't know how lacrosse works and it doesn't matter. He always has something to say.*

At first, Nate assumed that the Captain was still bitter that his son had rejected swimming. Despite pulling frequent all-nighters at the bank (fueled, Nate would later learn, by coke benders), his dad would still often wake up early to pull laps at the pool, or, on off days, to run. Nate was sometimes invited on these runs, and he went, but never liked them. The Captain always made a point of beating him, watching him from the finish line, panting, looking somehow both smug and insane.

Then Nate hit puberty, which, with the testosterone he was already injecting into his ass, was like extra puberty, and when he outraced the Captain for the first time, he tried to not make a big deal out of it, drinking from the water fountain with his eyes closed so that he didn't have to see his dad lose. "Got a cramp," the Captain said after. "Doesn't count."

During their next run, as Nate hit the route's final bend and began to accelerate, he heard himself gasp before feeling the pain in his ribs, where the Captain had elbowed him, hard. "Sorry about that, son," the Captain said, as Nate leaned against a tree, wheezing. "Accident. Meet you at the end."

Nate went running with his dad a lot less after that. And when he did, he made sure to let the Captain win. But always by only a little. So that his dad would never suspect. He never did. Quite the opposite. Sometimes, at parties, if his dad was coked up, he would put his arm around Nate and say to whoever they were talking to, "My son may be a lacrosse star, but he still can't outrun his old man. I kick his ass every time. Isn't that right, Nate? Tell them."

S2E11: Blog
Dan's POV

Setting up the blog was easy enough. I just hit up one of the math nerds from my old middle school. I could make my Myspace page look good but I couldn't do anything fancy, I didn't know Linux. Max had designed Gawker banner ads.

"I'll pay you in cash," I told him, pulling the bills from my pocket. "But you can't tell anyone." Max shrugged.

"Why would I?"

Max also lived in Brooklyn, but in a shittier neighborhood. The apartment itself was trash, but Max's room was nice, the only place where the AC worked. Plus he had this kind of Sherlock Holmes-y leather armchair. I envied him. Max was a beta like me, but making money bumped him up to alpha tier.

When I make money like Max does–real money–and I know I will–that's when I can stop stealing from my dad. I know that he knows.

S2E10: "Bonfire of the Vanity"
Blair's POV

Nate had been weird, but Blair had already decided not to say anything about it. Or, of course, she had said something, but she wasn't going to beg. *That's not me*. She did, however, ask her indentured servant, Dorota, to spy on Nate just a little bit. And of course she messaged *Gossip Girl*.

In a way, Nate wasn't acting weirder than usual. He was being normal Nate. Just like–more than usual. More of him being checked out when they socialized. They'd talk and she'd watch him just stare at walls. She'd be like "Nate," and he'd say "Yes?" And then, as if only just remembering where he was, he would smile. To reassure her. And tell them he was taking a smoke break. And be gone for hours.

Is he sleeping with Serena again? Serena, my best friend?

She knew it probably wasn't true.

Seal Stamps

Walter Benjamin wrote his best known piece, "The Work of the Art in the Age of Mechanical Reproduction," in exile, in France. It was 1936; Hitler had been *Führer* for two years. In lines that feel obvious and oversaturated only because they are true, Benjamin argued that "even the most perfect reproduction of a work of art is lacking in one element: its presence in time and space, its unique existence at the place where it happens to be." This singular presence in time and space was known as the "aura." Benjamin critiqued the fetishization of aura across Western art, not just because it ran on a scarcity logic–the aura is powerful because there can only be one of it–but because it inspired cultish worship, from reliquaries containing fragments of Jesus's toenails, to paintings by the Old Masters priced at hundreds of millions of dollars, kept in temperature-controlled freeport store rooms, visible only to God.

On a similar note, Byung-Chul Han uses "The Arnolfini Portrait" by Jan Van Eyck (1434) to analyze the use of signatures in Western art. While Western painters traditionally signed their names in the bottom right corner, Eyck writes his name in the very center of the image, which depicts a wealthy Italian merchant couple holding hands. In the background is a tinkling chandelier, a circular mirror–and a signature: *Johannes de Eyck fuit hic*, which translates to "Johannes de Eyck was here," or "Johannes de Eyck painted this." For Han, Van Eyck's signature establishes aura in a double register. First: "The signature lends the picture the character of an inalterable, definitive document. The date 1434 below the signature *fixes* the picture in time. Thus any alteration would amount to a falsification of the *truth*." But if the signature establishes the aura of the image, it also establishes the aura of the author, whose singular presence in time and space resulted in "The Arnolfini Portrait."

Han contrasts the Western tradition of signatures with the use of seal stamps in classical Chinese imagery. "In Chinese painting," he writes, "seal stamps themselves form part of the picture's composition. Thus they are not a paratext but belong to the text itself." Much like an adult coloring book is designed to be modified, Chinese paintings are designed to incorporate future inscriptions. "With areas of the picture left empty as communicative spaces, they directly invite viewers to inscribe themselves." While genres like stand-up comedy or fan fiction encourage audience participation, the distinction between author and viewer is still maintained. While fan fiction authors consider themselves to be "real" writers, they still pay homage to the auratic presence of the "OC," or original content, from which their AUs (alternate universes) derive. Of course, however seriously fan fiction authors take their own work, their writing is still considered minor by the broader reading public, not just because it pulls from existing intellectual property, but precisely because it is built communally. Compare this to *Farewell Meeting at Feng-ch'eng* by Wang Fu (1362-1416), which Han describes at length:

> According to a charming custom among Chinese officials, who were all men of letters, a friend, who is being transferred to another location, is taken to a beautiful country spot to celebrate his departure. A picture by Wang Fu titled *Farewell Meeting at Feng-ch'eng* depicts a beautiful mountain landscape with a pavilion where friends are celebrating his farewell. Each friend adds a poem to the landscape picture with a seal stamp. Here, painting is a social, communal act. Writing poetry...is a communicative event. It promotes sociability. Above all, it serves to lift the spirits and to entertain. Writing poetry is thus not based on the suffering of a solitary, poetic soul.

S1E12: School Lies
Dan's POV

When Blair put in a *Gossip Girl* tip, I was surprised. I mean, no one sees them but me. Even so. Blair likes to think she knows everything, controls everyone. I didn't think she'd ask for help.

"What's up with N these days?" the message said. "The girls want to know where Golden Boy's been sneaking off to...hopefully not seeing you know who again." *Soooo many people have told me to monetize this shit–but* Gossip Girl*'s whole power is that everyone reads her, anyone can submit, anyone who does works for me, in a way.*

By "you know who," I assumed Blair meant, not Serena (only newbs would assume this) but Lady Catherine. When the Archibalds were really cash-strapped, Nate was hooking up with her for money. Isn't that funny. A Duchess paying to have an affair with a destitute and underage aristocrat.

I rephrased the message. I always do. *Gossip Girl* was the one place where, people said, my writing really had its own style. They read it and instantly knew it was me. "Hey there, Upper East Siders. Rumor has it that Golden Boy has been sneaking off–where to? You know what they say. If you see something, say something. Xoxo"

S2E13: "O Brother, Where Bart Thou?" (Bart 2, the Brequel)
Chuck's POV

Serena and Dan want to fuck. But they can't, because their parents want to fuck each other. And that would be too crazy.

"We're connected," Serena tells Dan. "We always will be. But...I'm dating someone else now." It's true. She's dating Aaron, the young contemporary artist. Or she is for the next few months until, in a highly anticipated plot twist, she and Dan get back together again.

Serena hugs Dan good-bye. Serena pretends that she doesn't love him.

"Charles." Now Lily is begging him. "Please don't turn away from the people who love you. They're the only chance *any* of us has. Your father never learned that. I hope that you do."

Chuck takes Lily's secret file and burns it. This is his way of fucking her.

S1E10: "Hi, Society"
Gordon's POV

To his family, he had always been a kind of insane adult child. Everything that had been charming in Gordon's actual youth—his precocity and eloquence, the jumps between deep, immobile reserve and bolts of puckish energy—now terrified them, embodying, not just a refusal, but an inability to grow up. They were all in various facets of STEM, which made their adeptness at being normal seem evenly distributed and natural. Everyone made more money than him, of course. They always had.

When he started writing for TV (at least, the first time around), he'd figured that this would change. Now he, too, was making, if not well into the six figures, a comfortable sum which allowed him to not just live without stress but exist in a bit of style: picking up the tab for his younger, poorer friends; buying articles of masculine jewelry, plane tickets. He'd done it; he was a prodigy. He was less than twenty-three years old.

And yet, if he could sense that his family was happy with his success, most of what they expressed was relief—and trepidation. *Like, when would the other shoe drop.* Which it did, of course. It's not that he was fired for doing coke in the office bathroom (that was encouraged), but that he was messy about it. When the contracts were emailed out, he realized he hadn't been asked back for season six.

S2E17: "Carnal Knowledge"
Blair's POV

Beneath Serena's free spirit, she's totally conventional, just like I am. When I told her this, she said, "I believe in freedom. You always know I wish I'd been born in the sixties." But I don't mind being conventional. Convention is Constance. Convention is being the girls on the steps, is being Yale, is being Blair.

It wasn't until I started a rumor that the new teacher, Rachel, was sleeping with Dan (I mean, turns out I was right), got her fired, and got my Yale acceptance revoked that I realized: I'm addicted to chaos. By creating problems—in my life and the lives of others—I can avoid looking at myself.

S1E16: "All About My Brother"
Nate's POV

The first time it happened, I was alone. I was coming back from lacrosse practice with the other team captain, Nick. We shared a spliff as we walked back through Central Park, Nick peeling off as we hit the 83rd street exit.

"I'm gonna stay here and smoke."

"Ok. Catch you later, king."

It was spring, but cold out. Snowing almost. I didn't want to go home. I'd been smoking in the apartment, why not. There was no one else there. Using my navy blue Motorola Razr flip phone as a surface, I started to roll another blunt.

That's when my hand began to shake.

I'm just cold. That's what I remember thinking to myself. I was still in my clothes from practice, just my St. Jude's lax singlet and shorts. *I'll put my sweatshirt on.* But I couldn't zip the zip. My hands were trembling.

It was only later, as I looked for my keys, that I realized I'd left my weed in the park.

My mom was still in the Hamptons, where she'd been for weeks. She didn't call much. And I didn't call her. When we spoke, she said nothing. Just told me not to watch the news. "Don't believe everything they say about Bernie Madoff Archibald." I said nothing. I listened to her talk.

I'd long since stopped wondering why she was in the Hampton's instead of in New York with me. They hadn't taken the Hampton's furniture. The Manhattan estate had been enough to cover...had been enough for whatever was going on. I was just a beautiful transgender himbo, allergic to the intricacies of global financial Ponzi schemes. I just knew when things were bad.

I took out my Motorola Razr flip phone and texted my mom, asking for our family doctor's cell. "Don't worry. Just sprained my ankle or smth during lax practice. Want to make sure it gets looked at before the Yale scouts come in two weeks. Okay. Love you. Have a good night."

Then, I stripped totally naked in the living room, something I never did. I hated being seen with my clothes off, even when there was no one there to see it. I knew I was handsome. Even so, I loathed and was fascinated by the sight of my own body. They say the thing about transitioning young is that you get to be not just normal but regular.

It wasn't til I entered the bathroom that, catching sight of my reflection, I noticed that I had become my father. I mean this literally. I had my his body and face.

Part Two

A Dog Named Bark
Nate's POV

When Nate was little, his family had a dog named Bark. His father loved Bark. Bark was the son he'd never had. When the Captain would take a shower, Bark would follow him, waiting, at the side of the raised and claw-footed tub until the Captain exited, his weirdly hairless legs dripping, Bark lapping up the body lotion-flavored water that fell from his glutes and calves.

In the mornings, after his dad left for work (or "work," as they'd learn later on, the Bernie-Madoff coded piece of shit) Bark would cry like a human child. No one knew what to do. They got a dog psychologist who Mrs. Archibald had seen on TLC.

"It's his object permanence," Mrs. Archibald would say to her husband, quoting the dog psychologist. "When he can't see you anymore, he thinks you stop existing."

"No wonder he gets so happy when I come back," the Captain said. "Haha. My perfect baby boy."

The dog psychologist was an attractive Wasian woman named Julie who, after graduating from a top vet school, was now making bank as the Upper East Side's only canine mental health practitioner. She charged hourly; she and Mrs. Archibald talked for hours. It had seemed like a rip-off, even based off of tween Nate's undeniably dim understanding of money. Years later, however, he understood that his mother had been getting a two-for-one deal.

"Pets allow us to externalize our unconscious minds," Julie explained to his mother over Skype. Mrs. Archibald was sitting in the kitchen with her laptop, talking to Julie while drinking her morning *au lait*. "Does your husband assign his feelings to Bark?"

"Yes. Often. Even with little things." Nate removed a power-c Vitaminwater from the six pack in the fridge and poured it over a cup of crushed ice. "Like, he'll come back from a run with my son Nate—here, Nate." She grabbed his sleeve. "Tell Julie." *Tell her what?*

"Hi, Julie," Nate said.

"Without object permanence," Julie told them, "it's impossible to imagine other people—let alone objects—existing separate from ourselves. To truly know the other is to see them as both a love object and an independent being with the power to walk away. To have is only possible via the potential for loss."

"Wow," Mrs. Archibald said. "That's so sad." She laughed to herself. The tea cup of *aut lait* steamed, saying nothing. "Julie, why are you the only one who listens to me?"

Ideally, Bark was supposed to be able to develop mental pictures of the Captain, images he could keep with him in Mr. Archibald's absence. It wasn't until, years later, on acid and drifting through the Swiss cheese holes of his brain, that Nate remembered a child psychologist his parents had taken him to when a sleek and secret early transition had failed, to their collective surprise, to "solve" everything. The child psychologist asked him about his dreams. Nate said he couldn't remember them. Nodding, the shrink gave him crayons and asked him to draw something. Nate drew Bark.

When Mrs. Archibald came for a family session, the child psychologist asked Nate if it was hard to think of himself as a permanent object, since transition was, in some ways, the experience of his own impermanency: who he was (girl) had quite literally proved to be impermanent, even if it had been replaced by a new object (boy) which, at least in theory, aspired towards durability.

"When you look in the mirror," he asked Nate, "what do you see?"

"What do you mean?"

"Like, do you see a girl or a boy?"

He wanted to please, but also he wanted to be honest. No, that wasn't true. He wanted both: to please by being honest, the platonic ideal. "I see...neither?"

"That's so interesting," said the child psychologist, smiling encouragingly.

Even through the acid haze, he could still remember the imprecise contours of the man's face, that his name was Gary; that he'd known, in a vague but certain way, that Gary was a faggot, that this was in fact precisely why the Archibalds had plucked him out of the cascade of available child psychologists. Nate's mom had tried to find someone transgender, but, in 2002, there wasn't a single out transgender child shrinker in all of Manhattan, which was, for them, the entire world.

"So does this mean," Gary inquired, "that when you look into a mirror, you don't see a reflection at all?" At Chuck's house, sans adult supervision, they watched R-rated movies with surround sound on DVR. After viewing of *Bram Stoker's Dracula* (1995), he'd learned that vampires have no reflection; unable to exist fully in space and time, light just passes through them. The immortal, bloodsucking demon can thus be defeated, in the end, just by putting a mirror up to its quietly non-existent face.

"Of course I see a reflection. It's just hard to see that reflection as 'me.' I've never had any idea what I look like. I can recognize the individual features but can't make them cohere into a face. Let alone my face. I just see like a mask. Or blur." He felt anxious, suddenly. Like he'd gotten naked in front of his mom and Gary without even realizing it. "But I'm sure everyone feels something like that."

"No, they don't," said Mrs. Archibald, before Gary shot her a look. After the session, Mrs. Archibald took Nate to Dean & Deluca's, the upscale grocery chain which would file for bankruptcy in 2019, closing its SoHo flagship and existing only for tourists in global locations like Doha, Qatar.

"Get whatever you want," she told him. Nate was used to being told that he could have whatever he wanted. And yet, as a gesture, it still felt sweet. Overwhelmed with options, he got a ham and cheese croissant.

A few months before he was charged with securities fraud by federal prosecutors, the Captain went golfing by their Hamptons house. Because of Bark's lack (still) of object permanence, Mr. Archibald took Bark with him, keeping the dog on a retractable leash connected to his bag of clubs. It was hot out, weirdly hot for March. The joke was that, minus the weeping, Bark hardly barked at all.

The secret JP Morgan Chase business account that the Captain used for last minute redemption payments was dry, almost used up, *but no one knows that yet*, Mr. Archibald thought, removing his nine iron from the leather caddy. *Not even I know it, in a way. I want to know it, but I can't make myself. It doesn't feel real.* He tried to do like Oprah said and focus on the now. But the now was slipping away. *Don't think about it. Just think about this moment. Just this.*

Nate, who was shit at golf, was playing several holes behind his father when he heard the screams. Moving automatically, he got in the cart and went at max speed, which was 25 miles an hour. If he'd been watching himself on TV, he would have laughed: his father's wails, pangs of horror, and the small luxury sports vehicle, crawling up the land art-like hills.

In a reverse Oedipal twist, the real Mr. Madoff was turned in by very own sons. "I had more than enough money to support my lifestyle and my family's lifestyle," Madoff told journalist Steve Fishman from maximum security prison. "I didn't need to do any of this."

When Nate arrived, finally, at hole sixteen, his father already had a black eye from punching himself in the face. The nine iron head was bloody and Bark's skull was caved in with brains sticking out. That it had been an accident–the Captain lost in thought, Bark sitting, suddenly, within range, loyal and wordless–helped no one. News of the scandal didn't hit til months later, but even then, it didn't seem to phase him. He was already a broken man.

S2E3: “The Dark Night”
Chuck’s POV

People like to say that Chuck Bass is an evil guy. But that’s a misunderstanding.

Evil is real. It’s all around you. Look out the window.

I just describe what’s already there.

Befriending Hitler
Dan's POV

I hate that I'm like this. Like everything and everyone annoys me, an open wound that the world always wants to scratch. I hate it. I try to be a good guy. I love my family—Jenny, my dad. Vanessa, who's like my sister.

But somehow trying to be good just leads to being mad. When someone isn't good—not even ethically good, God knows I rarely expect that anymore, but when they aren't caring for themselves and just expect me to pick up the pieces, good Dan, kind Dan, perpetual sexless husband of the world—*how can I not get pissed the fuck off?*

I could be like Chuck or Blair, not caring for anyone but myself, a vacuum-universe. But then I would be evil. *I would hate myself.*

I wish I could be more like Serena, who could have a great time in hell, who would look at Hitler and find gentle, redeeming qualities.

Instead, I'm eighteen and yet somehow I'm already my father (the aggrieved one at the party). I wish I was Nate (hot, empty, always hooking up with someone). I've never known how to have fun.

Fans

Steve Vander Ark just wanted to make a space for other people like him: Harry Potter freaks. Vander Ark always had to be obsessed with something. He couldn't explain it.

At first, it was *Star Trek*. His first book, which came out in the eighties, was titled *The Complete Encyclopedia of Star Trek the Next Generation Season One*. It sold forty copies. That was fine. He was happy that anyone had bought it at all. It was nice to help out fellow fans.

Then his special interest in *Star Trek* faded. That was fine. He was like a tornado that had spun itself out. And even that in a way was okay. It returned him to earth again, allowed him to focus on other less consuming and yet somehow still utterly necessary things. Like not being broke: his full-time job. He was working as a children's librarian, in Michigan, in a town that had less than four thousand people. Something was missing, but no one would tell him what it was. He never made friends.

Then *Harry Potter* hit him. He'd just never felt like that before. "Something about these detailed imaginative worlds," he'd say, years later, at the trial, in a court recess interview. "They just captured me." *To let yourself feel the love you need.* "The breakdown you fear is the breakdown that has already occurred," to quote Winnicott.

The digital *Harry Potter* encyclopedia that Vander Ark began to assemble—eventually referred to as the *Harry Potter Lexicon*—was so extensive, detailed, and thorough, that it was referenced, not just by Warner Bros., which included the Lexicon's timeline of events in its DVD jackets, but by J.K. Rowling herself. As she said in a 2006 interview, the Lexicon was "such a great site that I have been known to sneak into an internet café while out writing and check a fact rather than go into a bookshop and buy a copy of *Harry Potter* (which is embarrassing)." In addition to listing and providing backgrounds on every single character, the Lexicon describes each location, creature, potion, device, and spell, in addition to offering its own, Talmudic speculations on how magic operates within the *Potter*-verse. Rowling described it as "a website for the dangerously obsessive; my natural home."

Then the series was finished. What was left? To some, it was the end, a dour rush of finality, not least because the epilogue, as many fans agreed, was bad. They'd come all this way with Harry; he deserved a good exit. Like all of us. Like all of us, but also more.

Vander Ark hated the epilogue, but that wasn't the point. The point was how many other *Potter* fans hated it, too. And if the book wasn't for the fans, then who was it even for? "It is amazing where we have taken *Harry Potter*," he told a packed *Potter* conference in Toronto in the late aughts. As the crowd cheered, its energy seeping through him, Vander Ark licked the mic and said that if people hated the ending, they should throw it away; it wasn't real.

"Expelliepilogus," he said. He realized he was whispering. "Expelliepilogus. Expelliepilogus! See! Do you see what I did there? That's a spell I just made up. It means—it means, 'Expel the epilogue.' And—you can."

"Expelliepilogus!" shouted a woman in the crowd decked out in Luna Lovegood cosplay holding hands with someone who looked like Ron. Black hair peeking out from beneath a scratchy, carpet-like red wig. *Can the world be what we need it to be? Harry and Ron just work for the Ministry of Magic, two cops retiring from their beats to do paperwork at the station and casually interrogate prisoners—this is where it ends up? After seven fucking books?*

"Expelliepilogus!" yelled the crowd.

"Jo's quit, she's done," Vander Ark said. "We're taking over now."

If you Google "Steve Vander Ark" now, one of the first hits that shows up is a YouTube link called "Harry Potter Lexicon author cries in court." Posted in 2008 (the year of the Financial Crash, one year after *Gossip Girl* hit TV), the clip displays the kind of lurid vulture aesthetics typical of a paparazzi era which didn't even know it was on its way out.

"It seems there could be dark forces at work in the New York federal court," the On Demand Entertainment newscaster tells us over a slow pan up to what could be—the Ministry of Magic headquarters? When Rowling emerges from court, where she has just emerged from suing Vander Ark—arguing that his effort to publish the Lexicon infringes on her copyright—she wears a chic tan skirt and matching tan top. The kind of wide, low-slung brown leather belts which are very in now. Big buckle.

"Vander Ark says he's been a Potter fan for ten years now," the narration quips, "and that the trial has been really hard for him, as he feels that he'd been talked into doing this by his publishers."

Projecting a diagnosis onto Vander Ark is another form of parasocial fandom, of course. *But whatever I've got, he's got it, too.* And yet—the special interests (as a basis for friendships, as a form of life); the impression of being a step behind the social cues; the loneliness.... If Vander Ark were a character in the *Potter*-verse, if this were r/Potter, would it be off-base to call him "autistic-coded"?

Like Katniss Everdeen and Gi-Hun, the *Squid Game* protagonist, Vander Ark didn't seek out fame. He was thrown into it accidentally. But unlike the other two, Steve didn't come out a hero. He came out the opposite. After Rowling cast him out, many of her acolytes followed suit, the parallel lines connecting fans to each other collapsing under fandom's ultimately hierarchical structure.

"He's been exiled from the Potter community," said Melissa Anelli, Webmistress at The Leaky Cauldron, a *Potter* blog, and one of Vander Ark's former friends.

"It's as if someone in your family had committed a crime," added John Noe, the Leaky Cauldron's creative director. "There can be no sympathy."

Vander Ark was never a communist, and if you look at his Twitter now, it's typical Boomer lib content: posts saying masks and COVID vaccines are good; D&D RPG tips; posts saying science is good. It's not that he's wrong, but who is he talking to? He simply misread the social cues and thought the Potter-verse belonged to everyone; that Rowling had made the work but it was the fans who kept it alive; that the countless Potter fanfics and fan artworks now floating around the Muggle world proved IP laws moot; that the ethos of sharing was good and the logic It wasn't that he was wrong. It was that being right didn't matter. As Anelli told The New Yorker, "it's [Rowling's] world. She lets us play."

S2E4: "The Ex Files"
Chuck's POV

The call from Mrs. Archibald came in the middle of the night. The first thing she said was, "Don't tell Nate." Then she asked for money, enough to cover the Captain's bail.

"Where is he?"

"We're saying that he's in Barbados, but of course he's not. He can't go anywhere." She began to cry. I was so used to hearing adult women cry. "I mean, he wants to go to Barbados for real, but I'm scared—scared he'll try something, or…"

"Of course."

"I don't want him to die. I just—he can't leave. But also I need him to disappear."

"Mrs. Archibald," I said. "Don't worry. I'm Chuck Bass."

His Ass, My Ass
Nate's POV

Which is worse: losing your fucking mind or becoming your father's clone? I turned around, looked at my ass in the mirror, and there it was—the weird, v-shaped scar on his left ass cheek. The Captain always said it was from sailing. *But who the fuck knows.* I looked at his scar on my ass. I looked at his ass as my ass.

I was either completely insane or I was Bernie Madoff Archibald, and most of America wanted me dead. Understandably.

I drew the blinds, put on my St. Jude's tracksuit (it was weird, seeing it on my dad, the fabric feeling bunched and staticky around my stomach and crotch), locked the door, even shoved up a table against the door, barricading it, I don't know. The FBI had seized our furniture but not the scotch in the liquor cabinet. Or my mom's Vyvanse.

As I lay on my sleeping bag, waiting for the drugs and alcohol to kick in, I thought of calling someone—but if I was my father, then I would have his voice. They wouldn't even know it was me. I took out my Motorola Razr flip phone and scrolled *Gossip Girl* until I fell asleep.

When I woke up, I was normal. Normal and regular.

The Good Life, *The Simple Life*

Aughts fashion was trashy, but so expensive. Juicy sweatsuits with Uggs. Von Dutch hats with diamonds. Paris Hilton in True Religion Jeans, low-rise. The War on Terror was flopping, American hegemony was in decline. At home, you could buy frappuccinos everywhere.

The era of stars who were famous for just being famous coincided, non-coincidentally, with the rise of reality TV, which provided a platform for these new "personalities." While reality TV technically began in the nineties with shows like *The Real World*, the genre didn't really blow up until the aughts, as programs like *Survivor* and *American Idol* became global franchises. While the US invaded Iraq, *The Simple Life*, starring heiresses Paris Hilton and Nicole Richie, debuted in 2003. This was before bimbo discourse; people just thought Paris Hilton was dumb. Retrospectively, we might say she played us. She wasn't dumb, just pretending to be, cooking bacon by pressing it between two irons, asking the camera, "What's Wal-Mart?" *What's Wal-Mart?*

In a lesson she would pass on to her protegé, Kim Kardashian, Paris taught us that the attention economy was just like the unconscious. There is no "no."

When the Financial Crash hit, the aughts tawdry luxury bubble popped just like the subprime mortgage market. The Chanel stores we'd shopped at were empty now. Or they weren't, but who could afford what we'd bought before? Paris Hilton, the girl who got it all without trying, was replaced by her former stylist, Kim K. Despite Kim's grindset, she had come from money, too. Robert Kardashian, her father, was famously OJ Simpson's lawyer; Simpson was Kim K's godfather.

During the aughts, the "the good life"–Lauren Berlant's name for the American Dream–looked newly shitty, void of glamor, but you could still get it cheap enough. Post-Recession, "the good life" was no longer good. It was just life. In "What Would AEI Do?"–which aired on January 10th, 2022–*Death Panel* podcast hosts Beatrice Adler-Bolton and Artie Vierkant critiqued the Biden Administration's "deaths pulled from the future" rhetoric. Within this catch-22 eugenics framework, the only people dying of covid were those who were already going to die young thanks to "pre-existing conditions." Being immunocompromised was a pre-existing condition. So was was being old, diabetic, poor, a child, asmthatic, or an essential worker.

"Life is a pre-existing condition," joked Vierkant, though it also wasn't a joke.

If we subtract goodness and life from "the good life," then all that's left is nothing at all.

Customer Service
Dan's POV

After his first day at St. Jude's, he cried. Not even after. He didn't even last the whole day. He cried during lunch, in a bathroom stall, like the most cliche fucking nerd.

"Don't worry," Rufus had told him. "It's just the first day and kids are mean. It'll get better. It always does."

By the end of his first month at St. Jude's, he was no longer crying in the bathroom stalls. Instead, he would cry in Central Park, where no one could see. He asked Rufus to let him transfer. He was only a freshman. He could go to another boy's school. He could go to Stuy with Max.

"You think colleges will understand?" Rufus had said. "When they look at your resume and transcript? Won't they want to know why you left halfway through your freshman year? Just try making friends, son. It's not that hard."

Rufus didn't get it. He had always been popular and hot. Even when he hadn't been popular and hot–or, at the very least, hot and popular enough to spin it. Alt rock soft masc. Gentle, handsome, discerning and shy. Of course, Dan had tried that, hoping that at least the girls would see him as a David Foster Wallace or Woody Allen type.

By the end of his second year (the bullying and isolation had only intensified), Rufus gave him different advice. "Treat the other students like colleagues. You don't expect friendship from someone you work with."

"School isn't a job."

"Of course it's a job. It's just a job I pay for in tuition dollars instead of a job that pays you."

"So then what do I do when people treat me like crap? Just ignore it?"

"Son, they're not worth your time." His dad was making waffles. Neither Dan nor Jenny could even really eat them this early. There was no time, plus Jenny didn't eat. But still, it was a comforting ritual: watching his dad mix the batter, pour it into their vintage-y waffle press with its shiny red exterior.

"Dan?"

"What?"

"I said it can't be everyone, right? Who treats you this way."

"No. You're right. Not everyone treats me like total crap. Some people just look right through me."

"Of course they do. Life's just business and in their eyes, you have nothing to offer. They're just trying to do their job: good grades and networking." He handed Dan a plate of hot steaming waffles. Poured maple syrup into a glass bowl and popped it into the microwave. Thirty seconds. "Don't take it personally."

"I don't know how."

"Interact with these shit bags like what it is: customer service."

S3E7: "How to Succeed in Bassness"
Gordon's POV

Most of the other writers were in LA. There were eight of us in the Zoom call: Marcus, me, the original showrunners (Barbara, Dave), two twinks from the reboot, and some viral teens that they'd scalped from the internet. I'd checked the teens out beforehand. "I can't compete with someone who's at 100k followers, Marcus. And who's also like five years old."

"You don't have to. You're not here to mirror them. Just be yourself."

We went around, did names. The two teens were named Nia and John. Both from LA. *Should I live in LA?* Nia was sitting in one of those driverless Tesla's that all the TikTok influencers had. The ones made from the same materials that Elon Musk had used to construct his villa on the moon.

"Are those the fires behind you?" Marcus asked, pointing to the digitized blur of flame visible through the windshield of Nia's Tesla X.

"Oh." She turned around. "Yeah. I should put my windows up, actually. Smoke's getting in the car." Marcus and the twinks (also LA-based) did small talk about how the fires had been worse this year, how they'd not just lasted longer (it was January) but extended longitudinally, hitting the Pacific Northwest and the border of Canada.

"That's why," shrieked one of the twinks *(they were in the same room, sharing a laptop, were they fucking?)*, "if we want *Gossip Girl 3* to capture the present moment, it can't deny our current state of crisis. The show has to embrace it. I mean what is *Gossip Girl* if not a messy bitch?"

"Apocalypse *Gossip Girl*."

"I don't know," Nia said. "I feel like shows whose whole goal is to capture 'the present' or whatever just get lost. The present disappears."

"That's so true."

"Ok, but the present has to be incorporated somehow," said showrunner Barbara. "This isn't just a show about rich people."

"The show has to be about itself. Then the present can just slip in."

I didn't even care that she had outclassed me within minutes. It was good. It set the hierarchy. Now I don't even have to try. Or I do, but I don't have to try to be the best because she is already. Also thank God there's someone else here who isn't an idiot. The real age gap between us is that you had to be hot and smart. I only had to do one.

"If we aren't going to hyper focus on the present, then we could technically go back into the past."

"Steampunk *Gossip Girl*," said one of the twinks. The other one nodded.

"That's such a good idea. How about: Steampunk *Gossip Girl*, but climate change still exists."

We went with Nia's concept in the end: a dystopian *Gossip Girl* modeled off not just *The Hunger Games* but *Squid Game*, in which the original cast returned, but as middle-aged adults. Instead of a semi-scripted battle royale, Serena, Nate, Dan, Chuck, and Blair would engage in what Marcus called "organic" combat over food, water, and other material resources; GoPro-like cameras, secretly implanted in the protagonists' cerebellums, would record and edit the footage for a coterie of overlords. Marcus was obsessed with it. Even over Zoom, you could tell he was losing his shit.

"You're a genius," he said. "Literally a fucking genius, Nia. *Gossip Girl* at the end of the world."

Since the network was billing us hourly, the Zoom call cut at six. Marcus and I went out for Burmese food after. I paid.

Demi Lovato Sings to Ghosts

We were originally setting out to search for UFOs and ETs. But then we came across this city called Vulture City, which is known for ghosts. I was scared, but I tried not to think about it. I put in headphones and listened to an episode of my own podcast, *4D With Demi Lovato*, just to zone out as the car drifted over the desert-y landscape.

We stayed in a cheap motel just for fun. The woman who checked me in said, "Are you Demi Lovato?" and I lied, "No, but people tell me I look like her all the time. I mean, like them." It takes training to see yourself clearly. When I stepped into the refreshingly cheap fluorescent lighting, stripped, and turned the shower on, for a second, blood came out.

You've been gone so long, I can't even see you in my head anymore. I have to look at pictures of you to remember what you look like.

We got to this creaky place because someone said–that's where the ghosts are. Matt Scott, who is a paranormal investigator and also like, soooo sweet, set up the EMF device, and almost immediately, it began to beep. It was like, the ghost could feel my energy. There was a ghost in the machine.

That's why I began to sing. "Skyscraper," my 2011 breakout hit. "Skies are crying / I am watching / Catching tear drops in my hands." According to British philosopher Gilbert Ryle, "ghost in the machine" reflected the problems with Cartesian dualism; the machine is the body, the mind is the ghost. *But that's just dysphoria, isn't it?*

I sang to the ghosts. I cured their trauma, and then we left.

S2E1: "Summer, Kind of Wonderful"
Nate's POV

Chuck kept texting him about the *Gossip Girl* hit. But Nate liked the rumor. It was an alibi. If people thought he was hooking up with a rich older woman, fine. It made her look bad, not him. The money part hadn't been posted on *Gossip Girl* (yet?), but even if it had, he wouldn't have minded. The real secret wasn't that she was older, married and paying him.

Fingering his anus in her husband's wood-paneled study. Summer holiday. The Countess asked Nate if he was still a boy. Nate's penis had been very expensive, almost $50k. The price for one year of St. Jude's tuition, or five new Birkin bags. The Captain liked to say that Nate had a Ferrari between his legs.

"Of course I'm still a boy. That's the whole point." He'd been so ashamed that he couldn't even tell her what he wanted. He had to text it to her on his navy blue Motorola Razr flip phone, looking at her face while she read. *Though I guess that's just part of it. Of our little game.*

I want to be able to do things for you that no other girl will do. That's why you need a woman like me. None of those Constance Billard school girls."

It was too complicated to explain that the trauma of real womanhood was what this was all about, where "this" was the fact that Nate was tied to the Countess's husband's Eames chair wearing the Countess's clothes, the Countess's thong around each of his ten thousand dollar testes. The room smelled like money when she called him a little girl. What was he supposed to tell her, that being forced feminized like this helped him process the trauma of being force feminized *as, you know.* He told her that this was just a weird kink. That, in a decade and a half, femboys would be a thing, Timothee Chalamet or whatever, they'd fit right in.

Big Fish
Bernie Madoff's POV randomly

When the Captain woke up, the first thing he said was, "Take me back to jail." He'd been a big hit in the maximum security prison. It was the last time he'd felt popular. He'd watch the other guys watch him on TV. Even the guards treated him like a celebrity. *That's right. Not just a celebrity, but a famous one.* The warden asked him for stock tips. *On the Upper East Side, I'm just another big fish in a big pond. Or I was. Now I'm the guy that everyone hates so that they don't have to hate themselves. It was just the Captain. It was just Bernie Madoff Archibald. He's the villain," they say. "Not me."*

Cowards.

Hypocrites.

Sometimes the hate in my heart is so powerful I can feel it. Congealing into a knife.

I don't even know what happened to me. I went to sleep in my cell and when I woke up—I was here. In a basement. In a windowless glass box. With Chuck just staring at me.

Victrola
Chuck's POV

Victrola was mine. I paid for it. When I go there, I can do whatever I want. And that is very, very important to me.

Perhaps it's worth briefly recapping here. Victrola is a burlesque club. Chuck buys it, at seventeen, in "Victor Victrola" (Episode 7, Season 1). He says that he wants the club to become "a place of escape."

I love my friends. But I don't believe in their reality. For them, the unconscious is a little locked box you can put under the bed and forget about. Not for me. I know the unconscious is real. And that you can't control it. The most you can do is admit what's there.

The basement in Victrola was already soundproofed. It has to be. I'd been using it—for after parties, raves, as a sex dungeon—for the past two years. The little glass room in the center of the room was where you'd go if you wanted them to look but not touch. Even the locks were already there. I just had to update the security system so that the locks only opened when I scanned them with my eyeballs. I liked that. It was just like Minority Report.

Max's House
Dan's POV

I didn't know what to do. I was at Max's house in Prospect Heights. We didn't really talk about the *Gossip Girl* blog's UX and now we were just smoking weed and eating dumplings that his parents had left for us in the freezer. Max was a junior at Stuyvesant now. He put oil in a cast iron, turned on the gas stove.

Sometimes it hit me that, for Max, Chuck, Serena, Nate and Blair, *Gossip Girl* didn't mean anything. They were just pictures and words on a screen. Stuy has its own rules, it's own social world. Max had a real girlfriend there, Dina, who he'd met at cross country practice. They both liked doing alt things.

And if, to Max, the Upper East Side was just an image, then to them, he was less than nothing; he could not even be negated in their eyes because then he would have to exist first.

"I'm just worried."

"Why?"

"That someone will figure out it's me."

"No one's gonna figure it out, bro. That shit is encrypted so hard."

"I'm not saying we're going to get hacked. It's more like—someone being able to tell that it's me."

"Ok, main character." Max finished scrubbing out the pan, put it back on the stove to dry. *Nate, Serena, Blair—had I ever seen them wash a dish?* "Why would anyone suspect you? Didn't you say that these people don't even know you exist?"

"I mean...they sort of do."

"So you sort of exist."

"Yeah."

"What's that like for you?"

"I don't know. Sucks." Max nodded, saying nothing. *Did he get it? I could never really tell. Sometimes it felt like we were brothers and sometimes he just seemed distracted. My words went through him.* Max reached around in his backpack until he found the grinder and the bag of weed.

"I mean, they know you're Serena's boyfriend, right?"

"So?"

"So what, cuck lord? Isn't that enough of an alibi? Why would Serena's boyfriend be snitching on her on the internet. And for zero money." *But that's exactly what I was doing.* I watched Max roll a joint.

"I'm not judging you," he said, finally.

"Yeah. Of course."

> A relation of cruel optimism exists when something you desire is actually an obstacle to your flourishing. It might involve food, or a kind of love; it might be a fantasy of the good life, or a political project. It might rest on something simpler, too, like a new habit that promises to induce in you an improved way of being. These kinds of optimistic relation are not inherently cruel. They become cruel only when the object that draws your attachment actively impedes the aim that brought you to it initially.
>
> All attachment is optimistic, if we describe optimism as the force that moves you out of yourself and into the world in order to bring closer the sat-

Lauren Berlant. *Cruel Optimism*. Durham: Duke University Press (2011)

Minority Report

Minority Report is a love story. Made in 2002–just one year after 9/11–the movie takes place in Washington, DC. It's 2054, and a specialized "PreCrime" police unit, led by John Anderson (Tom Cruise), stops murders before they occur. The program is enabled by three "precogs," who lie in a bath of secret pool water, telepathically predicting crimes. The precogs are human. Their clairvoyance stems from maternal addiction, a thin "crack mom" euphemism.

Forced to experience each future murder, the precogs shriek. They shriek in pain, thrashing in their Photon Milk Bath pool. Once their visions are uploaded to PreCrime's data base, the Precogs are sedated by a semi-amphibian nerd named Wally, who injects serotonin into their brains. The nerd is in love with the female clone, Agatha. He knocks her out, caressing her face. As the *Minority Report* fandom Wiki tells us, PreCrime saves "thousands of lives at the sacrifice of three." Decontextualized, cost-benefit analysis becomes horror, seeing your own blood on the wall.

If you love someone, they can leave you. You anticipate the loss to experience it. You live the worst thing over and over, hypervigilant, in case, one day, it occurs. When it does, it's a dream, like something you've watched on TV and are now seeing in real life. An unnamed PreCrime agent tells the nerd that, like terminal patients or inmates, the precogs have been approved for a long-term stay.

"How long?" the nerd asks.

"Sixty years."

At least they're not in any pain, Wally says to himself. *And they're together. Forever. At last.*

Minority Report has one protagonist, but in a way it has two: Tom Cruise plays John Anderson, but like any celebrity, he is also playing himself. The movie is about John Anderson, but also is about Tom Cruise: the star persona, the Scientologist, the web-like skin, the guy who does all his own stunts. Tom Cruise's talent is looking so normal that he seems fake. He exposes the plasticky manufactured sheen of norms, not by cleaving from them, but by sticking to the rules with a serial killer's rigor. The norm is revealed to be what it is: a fake, a statistical average disaggregating into its disparate parts.

The Second Time
Nate's POV

The second time it happened, he was taking a history test. He felt his hand start to shake. The room was so quiet. Everyone heard when he got up suddenly, mumbling something about a bathroom break. The teacher said, "Nate? Nate?" as he left class and then he just started running, clothes tightening against his body as he fled.

> we're laying in our bed looking at our hamster run on the outside of her wheel. we're mumbling incoherent things like .. " hamsters can't really eat cheese" and "I wonder how to many curry for hamsters without killing them". I'm starting to realize that most relationships are mirrors of yourself, and that the people who you choose to be around is largely dependent on what you want to see in yourself at that time. You gave me a nickname today " you're calling me ur panda now.
> Nobody has ever given me a nickname before .. well except my rich uncle who use to call me

Precious Okoyomon, "Look at This Picture of a Dolphin Penis on My iPhone." *Fanzine* (October 2, 2016)

Max's House 2
Dan's POV

I didn't even realize I'd fallen asleep. Just woke up and it was almost midnight. I guess I'd passed out. I mean, I smoke weed, but not like Max does. The TV was still on. We'd been watching *Minority Report.* I didn't see Max—I guess he'd gone up to his room—but he'd left a towel and a toothbrush on the coffee table.

If Max thought I was a loser for being such a lightweight with weed, he didn't mention it in the morning. We had coffee and Trix and talked more about the site. "If you think people will suspect," he said, pouring Sunny D into my empty coffee mug, "then write stuff about yourself."

"Like fake rumors?"

"Or real ones. I don't know. But if *Gossip Girl* is talking shit about you, then you're just a target like everyone else. You just look like everyone else. Plus," he laughed a little, "won't it make you more popular?"

"What? People making fun of me online?"

"All bad PR is PR."

After borrowing a t-shirt and a pair of boxers from Max, I got on the L train and then the 4. I'd told Serena that they could go for a walk in Central Park.

Later that evening, a new post appeared on *Gossip Girl.* "Spotted: S and Lonely Boy, out for a romantic Sunday stroll. Don't worry, we understand. Dating a loser can be comforting: at least you know he'll never leave. But even if you choose not to kiss and tell, we can still smell the boredom on your face. Don't forget, S: the Upper East Side is your oyster. Why not date another pearl?"

The thing about self-hate is that no one knows you better than yourself.

S3E10: "The Last Days of Disco Stick"
Gordon's POV

We were each assigned a character and told to think about the overall vibe of the show. It was plague off-season so flights were happening, though of course TBD, especially with the new water shortages, everything TBD. But Marcus said get to know yourselves, get to know each other, get to know your character, and then we'd all meet in LA.

"Why does everyone have to fly here lol," Nia texted me. "I'm saying that and I even live here."

"Lol"

"Not that I don't want to hang out with u but also lol."

"What did he even mean by 'vibe of the show' like how it's gna look and stuff? I'm like idk that's not my job ask the stylists u literally hired lol."

"literallyyyy"

"What ru gna say."

"Idk. I told him I liked that *Gossip Girl* 1 was kind of campy, like it was glam but it was the CW you know? Like Blair was always on her I'm Grace Kelly, *Breakfast at Tiffany's* shit. And with *Gossip Girl 2*, they moved it to HBO so it had to do that whole prestige tv look."

"Which is what lol."

"Idk. Like high production value and *Euphoria* lights. But also not fully because they were trying to make it look *Succession*-y. Like there was a hole somewhere that all the color was slowly being drained out of. It tried to be two opposite things and so just ended up confused, like a rich person without taste who just buys everything in the store."

In terms of character assignments, Marcus gave me Dan and Nia got Vanessa, which we were both lol about. He also told us that it was okay if aspects of our own lives bled into the characters, that it was okay to do a kind of auto-fiction thing. But I didn't want fictional Dan to be anything like me.

I could tell that Marcus was annoyed with my job performance, even if he wouldn't say it because we were friends. Also because it's just kind of an awkward thing to bring up? *Like, how do you tell someone that they're annoying at work.* My brain was a plastic bag. I forgot stuff. I gave off a weird vibe. Not really anything quantifiable until it is. Show up late to enough Zoom meetings and people start noticing. Marcus didn't have to say shit.

Jobs are usually like that for me. They like my resume, they think I'm charming, then they work with me for two weeks and are like, what the fuck is wrong with you. And I both feel them getting mad and feel powerless to fix it, *what do I even do differently*, car locked in a puddle of mud wheels spinning out. Not going anywhere. *I'm already trying as hard as I can.* And I can tell that everyone's looking at me and is watching me fuck up. *Not even idiot-savant. Just idiot.* Nia told me not to stress.

"You're doing good. Stop imagining bad things that haven't happened and reacting to that instead of reality."

"I know Marcus is mad that I haven't written more but I just feel blocked. Like idk if people should find out that Dan is *Gossip Girl*, or if he should even be *Gossip Girl* anymore. Maybe that's giving him too much credit and the blog should be run by an AI."

"Maybe he's *Gossip Girl* but then he just stops," Nia said. "And no one finds out and he doesn't face consequences. I mean, that seems realistic lol."

"But what would get him to stop? Like is it a big character development moment where he realizes something about himself, or is it just the fear of being discovered and like literally sued? Who even cares about a stupid gossip blog when their food supply chain has collapsed? I don't know. People always care about gossip, I guess. That's how information spreads. Maybe instead of telling us who's sitting on the steps of the Met, *Gossip Girl* delivers hot tips on where to buy water purification tablets wholesale."

"See? You've literally got it. Lol"

"Lol. whatever. I mean, thanks." I couldn't tell if I was blushing or just felt relief. "For real though. That means a lot. Anyway. What about you? What are you going to do with Vanessa?"

"Idk. To be honest, I kind of want her to just vibe."

"What do you mean?"

"I mean, she's the only main character who isn't white lol. I don't want her to just be there to prove a point. Or to just exist in relation to Dan and Nate. She deserves her own life. Everyone does. Or whatever life is left."

Then she had to run. She was doing some kind of TikTok photo shoot. I said that seemed glamorous and Nia said, "Yes, but I'm tired, lol," and that most glamorous things are underpaid.

Hot Girls
Serena's POV

Some trans men fail out of being girls, and some trans guys are hot girls. If it doesn't feel real, that might help you to do it better.

Some hot girls who are boys are great at monetizing their hotness. They monetize, but in their heads is a little voice that says, *whatever is happening, whatever they say to you, you're a boy. There's a place they can't touch you, and that place is called your head.*

Anyway, Serena was like that.

Victrola
Chuck's POV

Victrola makes sense to me. It's about money and it's about sex. It's about what we do for money: the way we beg for it. The way people beg me for it, I mean. And how that's sex.

Coffee Shop
Vanessa's POV

When Nate called, I was doing my opening shift at Rufus's Williamsburg art gallery/coffee shop.

"Vanessa. Can you come by?" He had been crying. I could tell from his voice. I'd seen him cry before. I imagined his eyes–the puffy red and white lids.

"Oh my god. Nate, are you okay?"

"Yeah. I mean, no. I just–I need to see you. Do you have time?"

"I'm working until six, but I'll come over as soon as I get off. Or–do you just want to come here?"

"I can't. I can't explain why, but–I just can't right now."

"Okay." Okay. *You're having a panic attack. Can you just deal with it. Not that I was trying to be mean, or saying that mental health wasn't real. Nate just never had to, like–just deal with it. He got to feel his feelings whenever he wanted to. In a park. In public. At school. That's all. And I knew exactly what he was thinking because he'd said it before. "It's an emergency. If you really loved me, you'd call off work." Didn't he know that I'd do it in a second if I could? There was a reason my mom only had one* Gossip Girl *cameo. The reason is that she's poor.*

After a while–I was cleaning out the espresso machine–I could hear him mentally and emotionally shut off, and I knew that I was talking to a void.

The Plaza
Serena's POV

When Nate called Serena, she was surprised. *But I mean, no matter what else has happened, there's always been a lot of love between us. Okay, we had sex when he was Blair's boyfriend. And that was really bad. But he's more like my brother. I can't explain.*

"You want to meet up right now?"

"Yes. Somewhere private."

She looked up from her Pink Razr Flip phone. She was passing the Plaza Hotel.

"How about the Plaza?"

"Serena, that's not very private. That's a hotel."

"Yes, okay, true! But! I'm also walking right towards it. So you know I won't be late."

When I met Nate inside the Plaza's lobby, which honestly looked so gorgeous (who else has chandeliers?), I could tell that he was frantic.

S3E13: "The Hurt Locket"
Dan's POV

Serena had promised that we would go for a walk, just the two of us, and not just a walk but a walk in Brooklyn, where I lived, versus the normal routine, me tailing her to various Upper East Side soirees, miserable, not knowing anyone. Serena had seemed disappointed that all I had planned was walking, as if there needed to be some other photogenic activity involved. "I just want to spend time with you," I told her. "So–to me, at least–it doesn't matter what we do."

"Doesn't matter? Don't you want to have fun?"

Maybe fun just meant different things to us. Serena liked activities. That wasn't bad. I just never knew how to engage. My dad and Jenny loved to play cards and I did it as a way to hang out. But each new game was a new set of rules to memorize and I would always forget. Jenny liked games because she was competitive, and Uno or Go Fish or was what my dad called a "healthy outlet" for her urge to be ruthless. I was happy for Jenny when she won because it made her happy. I could never bring myself to care enough about winning, so I'd lose.

"You do activities on a date so that you and the girl have something to talk about," my dad had said. "People are shy. They need something to triangulate with."

"I get that. So like watching a movie. And then during dinner you can share if you liked it or not."

"You've got it, son."

We'd planned to meet in DUMBO near the Williamsburg Bridge so that we could walk over it together at sunset. I waited and waited but Serena never showed up.

My Favorite Cereal is Special K Because of the Freeze Dried Strawberries

Gordon's POV

When Nia FaceTimed, I was alone in my room doing K.

"Hey, what's up? Do we have…" I looked at my phone. "I thought that work thing was tomorrow?"

"Oh yeah. It's tomorrow. I was just calling to say hey. Is that weird."

"No, no. Not weird."

"I can call back."

"No, now is good. Let me just...one sec." *Feel normal. Do something normal.* "I'm going to take you up to my roof." The K was hitting in a nice way. It was two in the afternoon. *I should eat after this. I should go for a run.* It was fall. I put on a sweatshirt on.

"What are you doing now," Nia said after I showed her the skyline, the clouds, someone's birthday balloons, one shaped like a five and one shaped like a two, floating up to nowhere now. *Happy twenty-fifth birthday. Happy fifty-second birthday to me.*

"I was...writing."

"Oh, nice. Like show stuff?"

"No. Uh. My own work."

"Oh, sick. That rules. What are you working on?" *Nothing. I'm lying to you. I was "working" on something in the sense that I had been for the past however many years, which is what all washed-up child prodigies do.*

"Just this thing I've been doing on and off for the past few years. It's going slow because–you know, work and stuff…"

"Yeah," Nia said. "I struggle with that, too." She was driving somewhere, the phone balanced, wobbling, on the dash.

"Where are you driving to?"

"Wait, what are you working on? I want to know."

"No one cares."

"What? I care. That's literally why I asked."

"No one cares because I'm old."

"What the hell?" The car swerved and so did her phone as it dropped off the dashboard and fell somewhere underneath the seat. First I saw nothing and then I saw Nia's toes, which were in platform sandals and socks, and then Nia's hand, which grabbed the phone, and me, before we slipped underneath the brakes.

"Sorry about that," she said, still driving, as she placed me on the dash again. "The phone holder thingy broke. I should buy a new one."

"Are you okay?"

"Yeah, totally fine. Wait. What were we talking about? Oh, yeah. That you're old. You're not even old though."

"I'm a full decade older than you."

"But that's not like, *old* old. Especially for men."

"So true."

"I have a call in five, though. So you should tell me what your thing is about before I have to go."

"Um…" The sun was starting to set. Spikes of light hurling themselves against they sky. *Each sunset is generic and beautiful.* "Um…have you ever heard of *NYMPHOWARS*?"

"No, what's that?"

"See, I told you.."

"Oh my god, you're so annoying."

"Because I'm old."

"The only time you annoy me is when you talk about being old. Also the way you dress."

"What's wrong with my clothes?"

"You just dress funny." *God damn it. God damn it fuck.*

"What do I wear that's funny?"

"Oh, you know. You love...you love a shirt with words." *I'm never wearing a shirt with words again.*

"Wait, what else is corny about the way I dress. Or in general. What else aren't you telling me."

"Gordon, oh my god. I didn't mean to make this into a thing." She rubbed her eyes and sighed. "Your shirts with words on them are fine. Don't go, like....throw them all out or some shit. Okay? They're very you."

"If I wear something corny in the future, do you promise you'll tell me?"

"Yes! I'll tell you. Okay? But now you have to tell me about your thing because I'm leaving in ninety seconds."

"Okay." *Calm down. Just be normal. Be normal, okay? It's fine. Nia likes you. No one is mad at you.* "Do you know Macy Rodman?"

"Oh, yeah. The pop star."

"Yeah."

"She's kind of like Weird Al except her music is good. I actually met her in LA when I first moved here. She was doing a show. This was back when I was broke and bitches didn't know me. And Macy like let me do a bump of her blow in the bathroom of this club. Literally such a sweetheart."

"That fucking rules. And damn. You really know everyone."

"I mean, it's my job," she said, and just smiled. "So you're writing about her?"

"Sort of. She did this podcast in 2018 called *NYMPHOWARS* with this other girl, Theda Hammel..."

"Theda? Like the one who made that movie?"

"Yeah."

"That movie rules. I didn't know they used to work together."

"Yeah, they're like best friends. I have all the episodes if you want them. I can send them to you. They're literally so good."

"I would love that. What's the vibe?"

"I mean, they were making like, weird stuff back when everyone either had to do influencer or 101 shit. But they were doing their own weird thing and each episode was paradigm-shifting but they were still considered niche. Like, the kind of mass market trans audience that we have now, that didn't exist in 2018. Trans people who were weird only started getting getting big on Twitter in like 2020 because everyone was online. Also a bunch of people came out when quar first hit. That's why Macy's 2021 album was able to blow up in the way her 2017 album couldn't, even though that first one also rips."

"So you're writing like essays about the show?"

"Sort of. I mean, there are some essays in there, but it's also narrative, and kind of a period piece. Of like 2016-2020. The Trump presidency, the anti-woke backlash that ensued. The story is about this guy who's writing a *NYMPHOWARS* fanfic. He lives in rural Wisconsin, and there aren't any trans people where he is. Just like one other guy. And, you know. That's not a whole world. So he becomes obsessed with *NYMPHOWARS* and Macy and Theda and befriends other fans of the show who live in New York, and at first it's good but then he becomes–kind of like a stalker."

"Wait. That sounds, like, good," Nia said. "I would read it."

"Actually?"

"Duh."

"Oh. Cool. I mean, thank you." *I hadn't expected that.* "I'll send you the episodes. Do you–have to go to your call now?"

"What call? Oh." She laughed and the car slowed. "I don't have a call. I was just fucking with you."

"Wait–"

"Don't be mad," she said, flipping the camera so that it faced the road. "I *am* going to go get In-N-Out though so BYE you can't even be mad!! Byee!!!!" She hung up.

S4E2: "Double Identity"
Nate's POV

Serena wanted to get high tea in the Champagne Bar underneath the chandeliers, and I didn't know how to tell her, *that's my nightmare. What if it happens again.*

"Let's just walk around or something."

"You want to just walk around this hotel?"

"I don't want anyone to see us."

"Okay. Whatever you need, Nate. I love you." She smiled. *If Serena could make it feel like an adventure, then she could make herself do it. And enjoy it sincerely. Whatever it was.* "Hey. Let's take the elevators all the way to the top. And then make our way down."

That's when the *Gossip Girl* hit must have spotted us.

Flip Phone of My Heart

There's no need to do close reading because the Wiki page states it outright: "*Gossip Girl* is known for its product placement. The show had a contract with Verizon Wireless for its first five seasons; all the characters were seen with phones chosen by the brand until the deal ended by the sixth season." The *Gossip Girl* blog gives the characters an excuse to be looking at their phones constantly; the phones (animated by *Gossip Girl*, voiced by *Veronica Mars* star Kristen Bell) become main characters. While Verizon's contract meant that early seasons are dominated by the Motorola flip phone (which, in many ways, became synonymous with the look of the show), by season five, both Dan and Serena have iPhones. The iPhone and *Gossip Girl* TV show both premiered in 2007.

While the Verizon contract ended, cell phones remained central to the CW's breadwinner, which, at the end of the day, was less about pushing one specific brand and more about getting teens to buy phones. Web 2.0–which relies on user-generated content and a participatory audience–couldn't function without smartphone saturation. To quote Barbra Robin, former VP of Integrated Marketing at the CW (she's now a network VP), "It was really about showing features on a device. Initially, it was just a wireless phone, but eventually that became a smartphone, a tablet, all these other types of technology that took them through their day and showed how they used it to get from one place to the next."

Interestingly, none of the original *Gossip Girl* parents own the means of cell phone and internet production. Instead, they own the twentieth century's infrastructure. Bart Bass is in real estate (Bass Industries); the Captain is in finance. The closest we get is Aki's father, who, in the *Gossip Girl* reboot, is a Rupert Murdoch stand-in.

Spotted
Dan's POV

The *Gossip Girl* tip came in just as I'd finally said *fuck it. I'm going home.*

"Spotted: S and N going for private tour of the Plaza hotel." A blurry cell phone pic of the two of them, king and queen of the Upper East Side, stepping into the hotel elevator. "Is this what N's been hiding all along?"

S2E19: "Doctor Estrangeloved"
Nate's POV

Serena didn't believe me.

"I don't expect you to believe me," I said.

"Nate."

"I–I don't even know whether or not to believe it myself. I just needed to get this off my chest–even if all that means is someone else knowing that I'm–having some kind of breakdown–you know?"

She stopped walking, turned around, and hugged me. Velvet carpeting. We were on the seventh floor. "You're going through a really hard time right now. With your dad and stuff."

"I guess."

"Well, anytime you feel...your thing coming on again, call me, okay? I'm always here." Someone had left their room door completely open. We could see inside as we passed by: the mosaic tiling, headboard encrusted in brocade, duvet on the floor.

"Thanks. And if there's anything you want to talk to me about, you know I'm always here." Her face went blank for a sec. Then she blushed, shook her head. *Her hair was beautiful. It had always been like that.*

"It's stupid. Especially compared to what you're going through."

"Come on."

"Well, actually–I'm glad you offered. Because there is something I wanted to tell you. Something that–something that only you would understand."

"Tell me," I said.

She never got to.

Thoughts
Dan's POV

FUCK FUCK FUCK FUCK FUCK FUCK FUCKADSF FUCK LITERALLY FUCK YOU HOW COULD YOU FUCKING DO THAT TO ME–

TV Show Concept

TV show concept: it's *Oedipus* but instead of running away from death, the dad is trying to get his kids to kill him.

TV show concept: it's *Oedipus* but he's your son. You named him that.

"Why does my own child not like me?" asks Penn Badgely on *You*. But also, it's not his fault. "It's impossible to communicate with babies." What are you meant to talk about? Babies don't even read.

"And yet," says Penn, "for the One, I would do anything." At least his previous love objects lent themselves to a fantasy life. Season 1's One was a smart beautiful girl who just needed his help. And when she rejected it, he killed her. Season 2's One was even named Love. But, as it turns out, Love was a killer, too. We fail each other's fantasies differently. But the baby is blank; an idea of a cipher; the concept of "child." He tries to project, but there's nothing to hold onto.

Penn doesn't kill because he hates; he kills because he loves. Or he hates, but love makes him do that. *Love and hate are the same.* Or so he thinks. *Just a different way of knowing someone.* Every fave is problematic because fandom is violent inherently. Putting someone on a pedestal? Don't you think that's a little....hierarchical?

In a recent tweet, trans studies scholar Colby Gordon described dysphoria as "a baffling combination of dissociation and hyper vigilance." It's not just spacing out. It's also being a snitch. Colby describes the contradiction as follows: "So much of survival depends on inhabiting a state of not-knowing, a preventative strategy of cultivating a fog that occludes the obvious ('I am trans,' maybe, or more likely, 'I would like to transition.') The other side of this survival mechanism is to know precisely how every person in any given room you're in feels about, say, the size of your hands."

S3E20: "It's a Dad, Dad, Dad World"

Chuck's POV

"What do you want, Chuck. Just tell me what you want. Please. I'm begging you. Money?"

"Captain–do you really have money to spare?"

"I'm an old man, Chuck. I'm scared of pain."

That's when I hit him. Just slapped him across the face.

The little glass cube already had a hand-cuff set up, conveniently.

The 2018 Netflix premier of *You* starring Penn Badgely, who had once played Dan Humphrey on *Gossip Girl*, also featured a very big and prominent glass box. Penn Badgley put things in the box, but not in the penis way. After he knocked Beck out, she woke up in the box. Safe. Where Joe could see her. Where Joe could keep her safe.

Before the box held people, it had held books. Books that were not just vintage, but antique. The box was temperature-controlled because the books were very fragile and thus needed to be handled with the utmost care. A book was a baby and and a mommy and a beautiful woman all wrapped up in one. Joe liked the box because you could keep people alive in there, watching them, as he does in *You*'s third season, through a baby monitor.

It was very funny to me: Bernie Madoff, hogtied, my little toy.

"You're scared of pain?" I hit him again. "Maybe you're scared of liking it."

I'd been sad, when the old man died. But god had given me another. Not that I'd ever wanted to anal train my own father. I hated him too much for that. Bernie Madoff was never my father. That wasn't the point. By not being my father, he could pretend to be my father, and that's how I took my real and pretend revenge.

A Nice Guy
Dan's POV

I'm a nice guy. I don't allow myself to feel anger at others. Only anger at myself. And with myself, I'm very violent.

Queen Bee

Blair will do anything to get what she wants. It's what makes her mean. But what Blair wants, which is everything, is impossible; and this, despite her nastiness, is what makes her a relatable queen bee, the tragic heroine of the Upper East Side.

In "Can't Take a Joke," Berlant describes something called "humorless comedy." The protagonists of humorless comedies "are all committed sovereigns who need things to appear a certain way. Humorless comedy is a comedy of compulsive sovereignty." The word "compulsive" feels notable here, since it casts the desire for total control as an unconscious, irresistible urge. Total control, like any addiction, makes Blair feel safe.

It's not very funny, watching Blair act like this. Berlant argues that humorless comedies "are barely comedic because the protagonists insist on bringing down any person or world that threatens their ambition." If we are all built relationally, such that there is no "I" outside its web of social entanglements, Blair seeks to be singular, intractable. No one will move her; she moves herself. In contrast, Xine Yao's *Disaffected* describes the racialization of unfeeling: who is allowed to not feel, and why. "One must be recognized as sympathetic," Yao writes, "to be deserving of sympathy from those with the agency to sympathize. Thus, the marginalized do not have the luxury of being unsympathetic without forfeiting the provisional acceptance of their capacity for affective expressions."

To maintain control of herself and others, Blair has what she calls her "minions." I'm serious. That's what she calls them, and what they sometimes call themselves. If it's too on the nose that none of the minions are white, they literally serve a white sovereign–realism drifting to allegory–it also just likely reflects Nightengale Bamford's student body; Cecily Von Zeigesar began attending the single sex, Upper East Side private school on which Constance Billard is based in 1988, commuting two hours each way from Connecticut. Demographically, the school is still mostly the same; it's meant to be that way, with tuition at 50k a year. If they really wanted to change, Nightingale-Bamford would be free.

In *Minions* (2015), the prequel to *Despicable Me* (2010), the titular, banana-colored beings search for a new boss to serve. "Without a master to grovel for," Wiki explains, "the Minions fall into a deep depression." On one reading, this is a surrealist twist: alienation and bondage flipped to ticklish glee so that a show about subjugation can become both suitable for children and a twelve billion dollar franchise, making *Despicable Me* the highest-grossing animated film to date.

On another, more cynical reading, the minions just show things as they are. Socialized into a world that naturalizes and encourages hierarchy, isn't there a groveling part of all of us that falls into a deep depression without a master to serve? In "The Miseducation of a French Feminist," Jules Gill-Peterson describes "the interior space that we so often give up willingly in the hope that power will govern us from the inside out and relieve us of the burden of being ourselves."

Blair's minions serve her, but they don't like her. It's necessity, not love. When high school ends, they leave her, and the *Gossip Girl* narrative leaves them. They have their lives.

S3E1: "Reversals of Fortune"
Nate's POV

My and Serena's phones went off at the exact same time. Which meant one thing: *Gossip Girl*.

"It's fine. We don't have to check it now."

"I mean, maybe you don't, but I do." She was right. She was a professional socialite. Checking *Gossip Girl* was her job. I don't say this in a derogatory way.

"Fuck. Someone spotted us here."

"Are you serious?"

"And now they're telling *Gossip Girl* that we're having an affair. And…" She winced. "And...I totally, *completely* forgot that I had plans with Dan. I need to call him, Nate. Can you–just wait for me? I'll text you." And then she left.

Pressure Points
Dan's POV

I don't know what happened after that. I just kind of lost it. *Calm down. Just calm down.* I tried the little self soothing techniques I read about on the internet. Put thumbs on the hinges of your jaw (pressure point): press. *Walk. Try to think about something else.* I couldn't think about anything else.

Without even realizing what I was doing, I called Chuck Bass.

Dead Ringers

David Cronenberg's *Dead Ringers* (1988) is about two identical twins: they are both played by Jeremy Irons and are both famous gynecologists. Ellie and Bev (both girl's names, noted) embody the fantasy of twindom: that you can both participate in an experience and simultaneously observe it from the outside.

Dead Ringers is also a fantasy about mirroring. The twins are different—in fact, they're opposites. That's what makes the whole thing work. Ellie is the bad boy who seduces the patients. When he gets bored, he passes the girls on to his twin, the two mirroring each other so tightly that the women (or so they imagine) never notice. Until, of course, one of them does.

Sleeping with the same woman was just a way to sleep with each other without actually doing it. No longer able to triangulate, the twins lose their minds. *If I knew what you're thinking and feeling at all times, then I'm safe.* If I implant a device in your brain that extracts all your psychic data and beams it back to me, then I can react to you perfectly. *Unless I am you already, in which case, it's perfect. But what if I can't be you.* The movie ends with Bev disemboweling Eli on a surgical table.

If there were an afterward, it would go like this: why do Daniel Day-Lewis and Jeremy Irons look like twins? Are Daniel Day-Lewis and Jeremy Irons twins? Are *Phantom Thread* (2017) and *Dead Ringers* (1988) fraternal twins? Both movies ask the same question, but in a different way. Set in 1950s England, *Phantom Thread*, directed by Paul Thomas Anderson, follows the romance between haute couturier Reynolds Woodcock—autistic-coded, asshole, metrosexual—and Alma, the foreign waitress who become his muse. If they love each other so much (and they do), then why do they always fight? Is this really it? Love? We can only be loved when we allow ourselves to be taken care of, but forcing the beloved into a position of weakness to put yourself in the caretaker role is textbook codependency. In *Phantom Thread*'s narrative climax, Alma gives Reynolds a poisoned omelette, and he eats it willingly.

When your lover poisons you, that's love (unless you die).

S4E13: "Damien Darko"
Vanessa's POV

I didn't like who I was becoming. But it felt like I didn't have a choice. My job just made me a bitch and I worked all the time. *Work work work and then when I wasn't at work I was just mad at it, mad at having to go in the next day, missing when Rufus was just my father figure instead of a shitty, incompetent boss.*

He knew that he sucked at running a small business and I knew he felt bad about it. Not that it was hard to figure out. He would literally say things to me like, "I should have never become a gallery/cafe owner, Vanessa. I suck at managing people. It's just not my style."

Ok then when what am I doing here. LOL.

I just keep hoping that Lily and Rufus get married for real so that she can just bankroll his life and he can be what he always was: a sexy house husband who used to be a rock star but isn't one anymore. It's not bad. It's good actually. It means that Rufus always has time. That's how we became close in the first place—I'd go over to see Dan, run into Rufus, end up chatting with him while Dan if ran out to the bodega. Or if we were all eating breakfast together because that's just like a thing the Humphrey's did. Eat waffles in the morning like it's fucking *Full House*.

That's what I liked about Nate first as well—he was full of time. He was beautiful and down for whatever. And it was fine if he didn't really do anything because he didn't have to. He was rich.

I was already off the train and walking towards the Plaza when I got his text. "Vanessa. I'm so sorry. I know you left work early, but please don't come after all. No one can see me right now."

Fuck off.

Being Chuck Bass's Best Friend
Nate's POV

They say you can't buy love. But if you're Chuck, you can. For Chuck, money is love. It wasn't that he loved money, though also he did, not just what money could buy (though obviously that) but just the way money looked and felt. There was a reason that Chuck (who, let us remind ourselves, is legally a child when the show opens, he's seventeen) owns a nightclub (Victrola) with strippers. Not just because he liked to see naked bodies and also touch them, but because he enjoyed the display of cash, the erotic flow of bills.

After Serena left, I didn't know what to do with myself. I was scared. Scared of becoming my father again. I couldn't be in public. I checked the time on my Motorola Razr flip phone screen. *Ten minutes.* I took the elevator down. *God. They really put a chandelier everywhere.* Blair had always loved the Plaza. I remember her telling me that if Manhattan was a movie, then the Plaza was her favorite set. Other than Tiffany's.

When the concierge asked me what room I wanted, and I said, "The most normal one possible," and handed him the credit card linked to grandfather's account.

When I got in the room, there was barely even time to feel what it felt like. I shut the door and locked it. My phone buzzed. Vanessa. Maybe in the new season, they would give me a Blackberry.

"Hey, just getting off work. Sorry I couldn't have my phone on me. You know how Rufus gets. So stupid. Not even like there's even anyone here to see me text lol. Anyway. Where even are you!! Lol. And what's wrong. Do you want to meet up?"

Thank fucking God.

"Oh my god, Vanessa. Thank fucking god. Yes. Can you come meet me? It's a long story but... I'm at the Plaza hotel."

Of course, that's when my body started to Jekyll and Hyde itself.

"Lol ur literally so crazy lol. I love it though. Okay, on my way. Where in the Plaza?"

Fuck. I can't see her like this. I can't see anyone.

I looked in the mirror.

I hated myself.

I was totally alone.

S4E16: "While You Weren't Sleeping"
Dan's POV

My favorite thing about *Gossip Girl* is that everyone tells me everything. I don't even have to ask. They want to do it. I've set up my life so that they want to do it. I mean, it doesn't always work. But if something's bad, I'd rather know. Wouldn't you?

Chuck asked me to meet him at Victrola. Normally, I'd never go to a place like that. Chuck thinks he's so cool, but Victrola is tacky. *Not that it matters what I think.*

"Humphrey. How can I help you."

"Chuck." I showed him the post.

"So? Just because it's on *Gossip Girl* doesn't mean it's true. You should know that better than anyone." *What the fuck.*

"What do you mean."

"Have you talked to Serena about this?"

"Yeah. But, you know. You can't always trust everything Serena says."

"Aren't you two supposed to be in love."

"Of course we're in love."

"Well. Then that's an interesting thing"—he picked up his martini and downed it—"for you to say." I couldn't read Chuck's face. I needed a machine that would allow me to read people's minds. *Google Glass but for thoughts.* "Dan, what could I tell you that Serena can't tell you herself?"

"You're Nate's best friend and Serena's step brother. If the two of them were seeing each other, you'd be the first to know." He reached into a small snakeskin briefcase, took out a little bottle, shook out a pill, handed it to me.

"Don't be sanctimonious. It's all natural. Just a capsule of crushed lavender and CBD to help you chill." He held the pill up to the rotating strobe. In ten years, we'd call this bisexual lighting, but for now, it was just flashing lights. Onstage, Dita von Teese was doing burlesque. Everyone knew that she had fucked Chuck when he was underage.

I don't remember what we talked about. There was a chemical taste at the back of my mouth; it was like I'd used my inhaler wrong, and now it was dripping down my throat. I told Chuck it surprised me that we agreed on so much.

"We want the same things."

"Hwat..." *Why was I slurring words?* "No. We're opposites. That's how we were scripted. You're the bad guy and—I'm not." Chuck laughed.

"Aren't you the writer?"

"Of course I'm a writer. That's part of my character arc. Becoming a famous writer."

"Then you should know about character development. After all, what's more exciting then hero becoming anti-hero. Anti-hero acting heroically."

"But at the end of the day—"

"We both love control, Humphrey. And we'll do anything to get it. That's why we're similar."

"That's not true."

"What's being a writer if not the sick urge to know what everyone around you is thinking and feeling at all times? And not just wanting to know, but feeling like you deserve to? As if, by knowing, you're somehow keeping everyone else safe? But you're not even keeping yourself safe, Dan. Do you know that?"

I take it back. Dita von Teese is really, really hot.

I felt Chuck put his arm over my shoulder and lead me somewhere, down the gilded hallway with it's Prohibition-LARP aesthetic, past the

VIP lounge that everyone called "the coke loft" and a room that Chuck opened with a silver key shaped like a silver spoon, which hung around his neck on a silver Cartier chain.

The Twink
Gordon's POV

The twink came at 10pm. He was a tall twink, upscale normal, loafers and shorts. "Do you want me to give you head, Daddy," said the twink. If he hadn't had a penis, he would have said, no. *Let me blow you.* He spanked the twink with his arm around the twink's throat, kissing him, taking turns fucking the twink and having the twink suck him off.

By the time they were finished, it was 2am, and when he asked the twink if he wanted to stay, the twink said sure, brushing his teeth before curling up and falling asleep, Gordon awkwardly big spooning his elongated torso from behind, like a little backpack.

In the morning, he made the twink coffee, yogurt with honey and toast. The twink ate quickly. "Sorry to rush," he said. "Just—you know. The trains."

"Of course."

"This breakfast is so sweet though."

"Oh. It's nothing. Where do you work?"

"Manhattan. I'm in admissions at NYU."

"Wow."

"I mean, it's whatever." He laughed. Embarrassed? Cheerful? *Why is it so hard to tell?* "So, what about you?"

"Um....I write for TV."

"Really!" The twink put down his toast, which was fully naked, no butter or jam, not even salt. "What the hell. That's so cool." Gordon had literally forgotten that working on *Gossip Girl 3* was a thing people might be impressed by. Even if all he actually did was go on Twitter doing Zoom meetings and watch Penn Badgely YouTube clips.

"What show is it?"

"Oh. Uh, I know this is weird, but I actually can't say."

"Damn. Like they made you sign an NDA?"

"Yeah." *It's always such a convenient lie.* "Do you want more coffee before you go?"

The twink declined, drained his mug. Kissed Gordon's cheek before walking out the door. *Fuck. I forgot to ask for his number. Well, I guess he's on the app.* It didn't matter; they would never see each other again.

By the time Gordon had showered and dressed, Rio was working at the kitchen table, frowning into her laptop screen. "Do you want some coffee?"

"Wow. I would actually so love some coffee. Thank you."

"Of course. Does Effie want? Did she already leave for work?"

"I think so. Let me check." While both Rio and Effie mostly worked from home, Effie was often out at various meetings, both the kind that meant sitting in square glass rooms and the kind that meant partying with clients but in a professional way.

"Yeah, she's gone," said Rio. "Sad!"

"So sad." Gordon put water in the electric kettle, flipped it on. He excelled at these minor, puttering rituals. His parents looked down on him for still living with roommates, but the truth was, he couldn't imagine living alone. He would have gone insane. And besides. Effie and Rio were his friends.

After doing the dishes, making iced coffee and scrambled eggs for Rio so that she remembered to eat, doing the dishes, and putting in a load of sheets and towels at the laundromat, Gordon sat down at his own computer and opened the scene that he and Nia were drafting up. In less than five minutes, he was on Twitter again. *Fuck.* He switched his laptop's WiFi off.

"I'm going to the roof to smoke for a sec," he said as she nodded without looking up. Gordon walked up the three flights of stairs and sat on the ledge, looking down: girl in bike shorts, leaning against a bus stop station and making a phone call; delivery man fastening a pizza box to his electric bike. He did a line of K.

By the time he got downstairs, the drugs had hit. He opened a new Chrome tab. *Here we go.*

> a graveyard. And nothing, including Rodman's twenty-minute Caitlyn Jenner impressions, is scripted. "That would be absurd," says Hammel. But, she insists: "We have never done *improv*."
>
> "We literally do improv," says Rodman.
>
> "It's free associative amusing radio," Hammel counters.
>
> "Improv? I *have* heard of it," says Rodman.
>
> "We sometimes return to the conversational format," Hammel clarifies. "But once you've loosened up the asshole, so to speak, of premise, conversation will always be a little uneasy. Because there's always the possibility that the ground could drop out from under it."

Charlie Markbreiter, "Nymphowars: an Interview with Macy Rodman and Theda Hammel." *Garage* (December 6, 2018)

By the time Nia texted, he checked and found that he'd written three thousand words.

"Send it to me," she said. "I want to read. Not rn though bc it's 3am here lol."

"Wait what? Ur not in LA?"

"No. South Korea lol."

“What the hell? That’s literally so cool lol. How come ur there?”

“Long story. Work thing lol. I’m exhausted, let’s talk tomorrow. Love you.”

S3E18: "The Unblairable Lightness of Being"
Nate's POV

Their parents had always made jokes about them getting married. Ever since they were kids. *Nate and Blair. Blair and Nate.* Photos of them holding hands, Nate in a suit like a child businessman, Eleanor styling Blair like infant Audrey Hepburn, fetal cocktail dress.

This was soon after Nate started his bootleg HRT and going by Nate instead of [redacted], so probably the adults were trying to affirm him and didn't know how and so just sexualized him instead. He could never tell how Blair felt. Sometimes she seemed out of it and sometimes she looked happy, like this was the only time she had fun. Did she need to be comforted? Or did she need baby arm candy, a dissociating shield?

One night, when Eleanor's gay husband Harold was drunk (this was before he was a divorcee faggot), they were at a gala, Nate and Blair dressed in their color-coordinated kiddie couples fits, when Harold said, "Nate, do you want a chocolate strawberry?" And Nate said sure, so they walked to the fondue fountain with its melting walls, dipped the skewered fruits inside.

"You should try it with marzipan," Harold said.

"Okay." *What's marzipan?* He dipped some in chocolate. *Tastes like birthday cake.*

"Can Blair and I really get married?" he asked as they walked back to their table. It wasn't even that he especially wanted to. He just hadn't known what to say. He wanted to make Harold happy.

"Of course you can. Whenever you want."

"Okay."

"What are you two going to do on your wedding night?"

"What do you mean? Like after we get married?"

He tried to think of all the things Blair liked. "We would watch *Breakfast at Tiffany's* with Serena?"

“Really? That’s all you would do?” He didn’t know why, but he felt himself panicking. “Isn’t there anything else you’d want to do?” He still didn’t understand it, even years later. Then he understood without wanting to.

S3E22: "Last Tango, Then Paris"
Dan's POV

What the fuck is Bernie Madoff doing here. That's the first thing I thought as we entered Chuck's sex dungeon. *Wait holy shit. Did he kidnap Nate's dad?*

"Chuck? Chuck?" Bernie Madoff looked desperate and insane. "Who are you? What are you going to do to me?"

"N-nothing. Chuck just..."

"Get me out of here. Tell my family where I am."

That's when Chuck hit me across the face. Then he unlocked the little glass box, where Bernie Madoff was chained, hands behind his back.

"Dan won't say a word. Now open your mouth."

"Please—" Chuck put his foot (he was wearing the newest Gucci loafers, the ones with the horsebit buckle) on the Captain's face. The tip of his toe went in between the Captain's lips.

"Open your mouth. Or I'll make you shit in your clothes again." Bernie Madoff opened his lips and Chuck spit in it. I watched Bernie Madoff swallow Chuck's saliva.

"Now, I know you think you're going to say something, Dan," said Chuck, turning to look at me.

"If thinking it's bad to kidnap and torture your best friend's dad makes me—"

"I know you're *Gossip Girl.*" God damn it. *God fucking dammit shit.*

"I don't know what you're talking about."

"Yes, you do." He unzipped his pants. "Your public school hacker friend is smart. Very talented guy. But he's not smarter than the Bass Industries security team." Chuck picked Bernie Madoff up. The Captain was on his knees. Chuck slapped him before putting his dick in the Captain's open mouth. Bernie Madoff's lips were so small that when his mouth was shut you couldn't even see them. Just a little slit. Muppet lips.

"I wanted to tell someone about what I've accomplished. I could tell the help and pay for their silence. But what's more fun than nabbing the boy who can't keep his mouth shut..." The Captain was gagging. "...and making him shut the fuck up?" Chuck laughed. "Why don't you join us, Dan."

"No."

"Of course." He let the Captain fall to the glass floor, gasping, before stepping out of his cube. I could see the Supreme underwear band beneath his Ferragamo trousers.

It just happened. His hands were in my pants.

"You can do anything you want to him, Dan. Anything." He led me into the glass cube, pushing Bernie Madoff onto his knees and pouring baby oil onto his old and naked asshole. The translucent Johnson & Johnson bottle with its pale pink cap. It was the only thing in the cube other than us and a silver dog bowl filled with ice water. Chuck spread Bernie Madoff's ass while I put it in. I choked Bernie Madoff while we spit roasted him, and then I came.

Part Three

S4E18: "The Kids Stay in the Picture"
Vanessa's POV

So Nate made me come into Manhattan. Just to flake. Because he doesn't understand how trains work. Or time. This is 2009. Uber pool doesn't exist yet. You can't just cab it back to Williamsburg, or you can but it's expensive, Nate only takes limos. His own limo, preferably.

I got off the L as soon as I saw his text and walked into the nearest movie theater. It was a rando AMC, but they were playing *Dead Ringers 2*. I hadn't seen it, but I'd read about it in *Cineaste*, talked about it in forums online. *My other social life lol. Haven't told Dan about that yet. I don't know why. Weren't we best friends? But I like having a world that was separate from him, away from the Upper East Side. Not that any of them would have cared. They weren't on the internet like that. They were only on* Gossip Girl.

To be honest, I was surprised that Cronenberg had even made *Dead Ringers 2*. No more nineties, no more indie cinema. *Eastern Promises* (2007) was prestige shitty, Oscar-bait. *A History of Violence* (2005) was dumb. But *Dead Ringers 2* was like Cronenberg's old stuff, minus the Young Reaganite looks. No, that's not true. It was totally different. The twins weren't playing in each other's corpses. They shared a single circle that belonged to everyone.

S4E22: "The Wrong Good-Bye"
Nate's POV

I figured I'd just rent the room out until I was normal again. But then it didn't stop. Me being Bernie Madoff, I mean. I just kept being him.

I ordered room service and asked them to leave it outside. The food at the Plaza should be good but no hotel food is good actually.

I didn't even bring any my shit. I asked my mom's assistant to buy four t-shirts, four pairs of underwear, four pairs of socks, one pair of boxers to sleep in, one pair of jeans, all from Uniqlo, deliver it to the Plaza, please don't tell my mom. Vanessa said, "You're hiding from me."

"Baby, I'm hiding from everyone right now." She stopped responding after that. I wonder what Chuck is up to.

There isn't anything to do here except jack off and watch hotel TV, which is always weird as fuck, the substratum of the hive mind's dream. After day three, I asked Chuck to send an ounce of weed gummies to the room which he did, no questions. It was day four that I turned on the hotel TV and saw famous affect theorist Lauren Berlant.

I was high as fuck when it happened. I thought it was just a weird hotel channel, some PBS shit. But then it was this kind of kooky old non-binary person saying my name. *Why is the TV saying that?* They were in a room and yet also seemed to be outside.

"What?"

"I'm sorry, Nate. I didn't mean to talk at you."

"It's fine,"

"I'm Lauren. I'm dead."

"I'm my dad right now."

"Okay."

Forgiveness

In Judaism, there are three stages of forgiveness. While Christianity argues that we should turn the other cheek regardless of why and how hard we've been punched in the face, the principle of *mechilah* argues that forgiveness is not unconditional. Instead, the sinner must take accountability for what they have done, not just on behalf of whoever they've hurt, but for the good of the broader community, which might otherwise be forced to suffer repetitions of that same harm.

Selichah, the second level of forgiveness, is more narrative. While *mechilah* focuses on the harm, *selichah* is about intentions, the character's backstory, understanding why they did what they did, that their act was wrong but also that they have suffered. Like you, they are human and thus frail. Significantly, those who have been harmed deeply are not morally required to feel *selichah* for their antagonists; the Jewish God does not need you to love your enemy.

And this is because *kapparah*—atonement, the total negation of a person's sins, forgiveness, it's all wiped clean—can only be done by God. No human can truly forgive another. You can't reverse my sins and I can't reverse yours. This is the other reason why true love is to some extent impersonal: because true love is God's love. And God is inhuman.

If it seems depressing to acknowledge the limitations of your own capacities, then you're not getting it. *Kapparah* frees us. You aren't relieved of agency, of obligation to yourself and others (*mechilah*); but in the final moment of Judgment, it's up to God, it's out of your control (*kapparah*), as so many things are, this is a blessing.

So Annoying
Dan's POV

People were always telling Dan Humphrey, "You're annoying as fuck." Or they didn't tell him. That was the problem. They just dipped. If someone just told him in a chill, non-aggressive way, that would rule. No one wants to be annoying. Literally no one. If someone said, "Hey Dan, I love you literally so much, but you're info-dumping about Ernest Hemingway and I'm too tired to input the information into my brain right now lol," then he would stop info-dumping in that instant. Because at the end of the day he was a nice guy, or he was trying to be, and he wanted to make people happy, or he wanted to want that.

But there is no language to express annoyingness, even though it should be as easy and impersonal as telling someone that they've stepped on your shoe. But there is no impersonal, collective linguistic case. "Society?" said Margaret Thatcher as neoliberalism ascended. "There...is no such thing! There are individual men and women and there are families." We have language for personal conflict and language for the most macrostructural abuse, but nothing for what happens in between. You can leave society, but it never leaves you.

The personal is not inherently good. The impersonal is not inherently bad. Dissociation is impersonal, as are tone indicators, and (per Lauren Berlant) as is personhood itself. They wrote about this all the time. I wish I could talk to them about it, but they're dead. Death is impersonal. Except when it happens to you, then it's personal. "Identity," writes Berlant in *Desire/Love* (published in 2012, just one year after *Cruel Optimism*, their most famous work), "might be defined as the kind of singularity that an individual is said to have: paradoxically, identity is also the individual's point of intersection with membership in particular populations or collectivities." Berlant makes a similar point in *The Queen of America Goes to Washington City* (1997), in the wake of the Clinton/Lewinsky scandal, which they were obsessed with. "The experience of social hierarchy is intensely individuating, yet it also makes people public and generic: it turns them into kinds of people who are both attached to and under-described by the identities that organize them."

But if Berlant's work fixates on the impersonality of personhood, it was also fascinated by what they famously called the "intimate public sphere." This was also a Clinton/Lewinsky-era concept, developed as America wondered who maybe had or hadn't licked the president's dick. The "welfare state" was being slashed but no one could bring themselves to care, enthralled and imbued with a sense of national belonging as they watched the spectacle unfurl. Thanks to Monica and Bill, America was fucking itself. Contorting its spinal cord so that it could give itself head.

For Berlant, the Reagan years thus deliberately inverted American citizenship, as the "public" was now defined by matters formerly regulated to the domestic sphere: abortion, pornography, homosexuality. This wasn't a historical accident; as the seventies progressed, backlash to sixties radicalism coagulated. "A reactionary response grew dominant, which claimed that, in valuing national criticism over patriotic identification, and difference over assimilation, sixties radicals had damaged and abandoned the core of U.S. society. A conservative coalition formed whose aim was the privatization of U.S. citizenship."

What did this look like aesthetically and ideologically? Berlant describes the eighties as simultaneously anti-federalist and hyper-nationalistic, Bruce Springsteen-style American propaganda pumped out to obscure that actual federal programs were being sold for it parts. "The expansion of a mass-mediated space of opinion formation... [positioned] citizens as isolated spectators to the publicity that claims to represent them." Attachment, not just to America but to normativity itself, had become its own aesthetic LARP, "a rhetorical shift from a state-based and thus political identification with nationality to a culture-based concept of the nation as a site of integrated social membership."

Jenny was annoying but she also (not always, but sometimes!) managed to make it work. If Dan missed social cues, Jenny picked them out of hyper-vigilance. Like Dan, she was competitive; unlike Dan, she wasn't ashamed of that, which made it easier for her to execute. Like Dan, her annoyingness stemmed, in part, from class: from not having it and not just wanting it but wanting so badly that the want shines through every attempted performance of seamlessly Not Giving a Fuck, the B.O. of upper-middle-class aspiration that everyone can smell but you. Both Humphrey kids hated themselves. They hated you and yet they wanted your approval desperately.

S2E8: "Pret-a-Poor-J"

The character of Jenny Humphrey was played by Taylor Momsen, whose life was both generic and insane. She started working full-time at two years old. On her Wiki page, Momsen is quoted as saying, "My parents signed me up with Ford Modeling at the age of two. No two-year-old wants to be working, but I had no choice. My whole life, I was in and out of school. I didn't have friends. I was working constantly and I didn't have a real life." What counts as "real" life?

Whatever "real" was, Momsen didn't have it. The real, or one version of it, was taken from her. Her breakout role was as Cindy Lou Who in *How the Grinch Stole Christmas* (2000), which was shot on the Universal Studios backlot behind the house from *Psycho*. It took eight hours for Jim Carrey to get into Grinch make-up, which enraged him. Lead make-up Kazu Hiro remembers repeatedly going on break and returning to find that Carrey had destroyed his face prosthetics, kicked a dent in the trailer wall, and stormed off set. "After two weeks," he said, "we only could finish three days' worth of shooting schedule."

Momsen is good as Jenny because she was never really into the role and that works for the character. Jenny's vibe is slacker/baddie wannabe/girl who gets wasted but in like a *Nylon* mag way. Serena is a blonde, but it looks natural; Jenny wants you to know that she dyed it. Both onscreen and off, Momsen wears bowler hats, leather jackets, heavy eyeliner, and tulle. "Acting is easy," she told a publication called *Digital Spy* in 2011. "I've been doing it for so long and I totally love it. But you're playing a character instead of yourself." As Jenny, she was trying to access the real and she was running from it, just like any of us.

S2E18: "The Age of Dissonance"
Nate's POV

Famous affect theorist Lauren Berlant stood there on one leg like a flamingo. "Do you want to get out of here?"

Do you mean you want to leave the TV?

"No, I mean both of us, together."

I can't go anywhere. I'm Bernie Madoff. I should be in jail right now. If they see me, they'll arrest me on the street.

"How'd you get out of jail?"

I didn't. He's still there. I'm just also him. I just keep turning into him. Like physically. I don't know why.

"It's from your blockers."

What?

"The expensive bootleg shit your parents got for you in the nineties."

That doesn't make any sense.

"It doesn't have to."

I realized then that I'd been speaking to Lauren Berlant without opening my mouth.

Are you reading my mind?

"No. I'm not listening to anything you don't want me to tell me. I wouldn't do that to you. This is just how you talk to the dead."

Oh. I'm sorry.

It was still raining—it was raining harder, in fact. Lauren Berlant reached into their pocket, looking for something. They were dressed kind of non-binary Eileen Fisher, but it worked for them. Ruched shirt.

Long black flow-y jacket thing. Black linen pants. Short curly silver hair. Statement glasses in neutral tones. Quirky Gandalf Boomer vibes.

"Here we go." Reaching through the screen, they handed me one of those primary-colored propeller hats that child actors and cartoons wear. "I have one, too," Lauren said, pulling it over their skull and flicking the plastic blade. The propeller rotated. "I love funny hats."

I wondered what my friends were up to, and if I still had a family. I didn't, in a way. It was freeing and free fall. I put my hat on and ate the last three weed gummies from Chuck

"The hats are important. It's how we get into your unconscious mind."

Then a whirlpool opened up in the middle of the bedroom floor, except the water was the room itself, like someone had applied a FaceTune blur tool, w*ho Vitamixed the Plaza*, Lauren stepped out of the TV and took my hand and said, "Is this okay for you?"

Yes.

Here we go.

S4E8: "Juliet Doesn't Live Here Anymore"
Gordon's POV

When I got the call, I was alone in my room doing K.

"Hey, what's up?"

"Are you busy now? What are you doing?" She sounded stressed.

"Um, nothing. Just work. What about you?"

"Wow. Working late. What are you working on."

"Just…" *Fuck. I was k-holing.* "Some stuff for the show. What are you up to? What time is it in LA?"

"Shit. I forgot about the time difference. It's only ten here but it's one a.m. where you are."

"It's fine. I mean, I'm awake."

The K was making the room feel spinny. I got into bed, flipped the AC on.

"I tried calling my other friends," Nia said, "but they're all at this Echo Lake party that I didn't want to go to because I like–might have COVID?"

"What the fuck?"

"Yeah. I got exposed last night. It sucks. I mean, I feel fine. I probably don't have it."

"Yeah."

"Being in the house all day made me feel crazy though, so I decided to go for a walk and now–this guy is like. Following me."

"What the hell? Are you near your car?"

"No. I was manic and really went for a walk." I had no idea what LA looked like. Most of what I knew was from listening to Lana Del Rey.

"Do you want to um...what's the word for it. Call a car."

"I don't want to stop walking right now." *I hope the K isn't making me stupid.*

"How about you um. Call a car. And then walk around the block. And then the car can like come find you, and I'll like stay on the line."

"Okay." I checked Twitter. Nothing. Just kidding. I had lost two followers. *And for once? And for what*? "Sorry. I'm back."

"Hey."

"I was just looking to see how far away he was."

"How far is he?"

"I mean, I can see his face. He's just some random white guy."

"I'll punch him in the throat."

"I'm going to call a car now. Just keep talking to me."

Get out of bed. Get a glass of water. You'll feel better when you do. How to get out of bed though. I shut my eyes. "How did you....how did you first get into *Gossip Girl*. Weren't you like a fetus when the original show came out."

"One sec." It was less willpower then stupid luck which got me out up. Effie was gaming on our flat screen TV. She paused to watch me stumble towards the sink.

"Are you okay?"

"Yeah, yeah. Just um..." I pointed to my Air Pods. "On. The phone."

"Okay. Let me know if you need anything."

"Thanks." She unpaused the game and went back to slaughtering Guys with a retractable chain saw which unfurled like a ribbon, swinging across the desiccated steampunk landscape.

"Hey, I'm back," Nia said. "Sorry. The car's going to come in five."

"That's good."

"What did you ask me again?" *I couldn't even remember.* "Oh right. You asked me how I got into *Gossip Girl.*" She laughed. "I got into *Gossip Girl* because I was a fucking nerd."

"You? A nerd? Impossible."

"It's totally true." It actually did seem impossible though. Nia had many jobs, but her true job was to be cool professionally, to generate a persona that her fans, collectors, readers, and Onlyfans subscribers, could para-socially attach to and consume, cannibalistically. They wanted to eat her alive. They wanted to barbecue her and eat the meat off the bones and then display the bones in their rooms as mementos. *Fuck them. Fuck those fucking pieces of shit.*

"Okay. When were you a nerd though."

"I don't know. All my life? I mean, I'm still a nerd, I just figured out how to be hot as well. But when I was a kid, I didn't know how. And also I was weird-looking. Had braces and big glasses. True nerd shit. I grew up with just my dad and my older sister, but he worked a lot, so when I'd come home, I'd just watch TV. And like, for some reason, *Gossip Girl* was always on."

"So random."

"We had the CW. I don't know. So yeah I watched a ton of *Gossip Girl* as a kid, and then when I was old enough to use my dad's computer, all I wanted to do was go on *Gossip Girl* fandom forums."

"Damn. What was that like."

"I mean… One sec. God. Is he really still following me? That's commitment."

"I'm gonna punch his throat."

"Haha. Yeah do it. Yeah. Uh. I mean, I mean, the forums were good? Like that's how I made my first friends. I was a loser, I didn't have friends at school. I don't know. I'm like, very autistic secretly? *Gossip Girl* was my special interest. I only cared about *Gossip Girl*. That's all I wanted to talk about. So the forums were perfect. Everyone else was there for *Gossip Girl*, too. Well, that and pretending to also be fourteen so that they could talk to minors."

"Wait," I said. "What the hell." Nia's voice was a disembodied entity that filled the room like air. Nia's voice was a balloon. "Those forums were full of freaks. My first boyfriend turned out to be a forty-five year old who said he was also fourteen. He'd make me send him nudes and would send them back and in the pictures he looked like another kid. That still freaks me out to think about. Like, where did he get those pictures from? Were they nudes that another kid was sending him? Wait. Here's my car."

S4E21: "Shattered Bass"

In the original *Gossip Girl* pilot, Chuck Bass tries to rape two girls. First Serena, in the kitchen of his father's hotel. It's premeditated; he clears out the kitchen staff so that no one will be there. She gets away, but just barely. Later that night, at Blair's party, Chuck (annoyed at being rebuffed? Because he's just like this?) tries to assault fifteen-year-old Jenny, taking her up to the roof so that no one will hear her scream. Because this is a YA TV show from the aughts, she is saved just in time, Serena and Dan busting through the door, grabbing her, Dan awkwardly sucker-punching Chuck in the throat.

Chuck doesn't apologize for either incident. The show tries to redeem him, but this redemption doesn't involve accountability, just a more in-depth look at his interior life and a romance plot with Blair. Love, supposedly, has cleaned him, turned him around. But maybe the writer's room was just riffing off reality. By 2018, Ed Westwick, the actor who plays Chuck Bass, was facing four accusations of rape, all which he denied. Nothing came of it. "Beyond the statute of limitations." Same extremely old thing.

S5E1: "Yes, Then Zero"
Dan's POV

He took the train to Max's house numb, not able to think, he was having a panic attack. He forgot to even tell Max he was coming over, just showed up, then had to wait twenty minutes, milling around the stoop, while Max got back from the orthodontist.

"Chuck found out. About *Gossip Girl*."

"No."

"Yes, dude, I'm serious. I mean, it wasn't him. It was the Bass Industries security team."

Max sat down on his bed. *Not looking at me.* He reached down, pulled out a Nike shoebox from under his bed. "Want one?" he said, then crushed up one of the pills and snorted it. "What's Chuck's stake in this."

"I don't know. His whole family loves this spying shit. Chuck's dad used to keep files on people. Hire guys to follow his wife around. He used to have people follow Serena, too."

"So why'd he tell you?"

"I don't know."

"What the *fuck*." Max absently picked up the Spongebob stuffed animal on his bed. Held it in a way that was half hug, half strangling. The cloth yellow sponge face moving in and out like breath. "I don't even feel like the site has been coming for him that much. I didn't even know he cared what it said."

"Could just be some sort of power play."

Max sat up. He began to pace around the room. Those are actually the words that came to me, the stock phrase people use in novels to express a character's psychic distress at a moment of narrative tension. *He began to pace around the room.* When he turned to face me again, he was furious.

"You're hiding something." He looked frantic. Scared and scary. The label on his pill bottle, squatting below a *Neon Genesis Evangelion* poster, said Adderall, 20 mg.

"I'm not."

"You are. I can tell that you are. And I need you to tell me, Dan. Because we have a lot on the line here. I have a lot on the line. *I*..." He looked around, then lowered his voice. "My parents can't find out about this. My bosses can't find out about this. I work, Dan."

"Oh, you think my dad won't care?"

"It's not like that," said Max. "I like work real jobs. Under the table. Tech stuff. My parents need the money."

"Right. I'm sorry, I didn't thi–"

"It's fine," he said, embarrassed. "It's just–why I really need you to tell me whatever you know. So that we can stay on top of this."

"I...." *Could I even tell Max, though? Would he even believe me?* "Chuck told me a secret. Of his. Or, I found out by accident. That's when he told me he knew about *Gossip Girl*. Blackmail. To keep me quiet."

"What's the secret." *Think. Think, you fucker. Aren't you supposed to be a writer. Make some shit up. It had been a big deal for me, life-wise, when I realized that I didn't have to tell the truth all the time.*

"Chuck is gay," I said. "I caught him hooking up with another guy."

"*Damn*," said Max. He laughed. "I mean, it's not a surprise. That guy's into weird fucked-up sex and everyone knows it."

"Yeah. He's a freak."

"Who was the other guy?"

"I don't know. I didn't recognize him, at least. Just seemed like some random dude."

"Where did you see this happen?"

"At Victrola."

"Chuck's club? What were you doing there?" It was raining outside. It felt like it had been raining for days.

"He–he said he wanted to talk about Serena. So of course I showed up. I figured that, even if it was nothing, I'd get a tip for *Gossip Girl*."

Max exhaled. Lay down on his bed (Spongebob sheets, Spiderman duvet) took out another pill, and didn't grind it, just swallowed it dry.

"Thank you for being honest with me. I get–why you weren't sure if you should tell at first."

"Yeah. Of course."

"You know that we're still going to have to shut down the site, right."

"What?"

"Absolutely." As Max brushed back the hair from his face, I noticed that his fingers were shaking. "If Bart Industries is on it, it's over. They do security for Amazon. Who knows what else they have on us. It's over, Dan." *Fuck. Fuck. Fuck fuck fuck fuck fuck. God fucking damnit. Fuck. No.*

"You're right," I said.

Max got up, stumbled over to his bedroom window, and cracked it. The rain was still coming down. Rain dotted the windowsill like sweat. He picked up the half-smoked joint on an ashtray we'd gotten together when we went to Coney Island. A cartoon hot dog, erect as a penis, holding up the Nathan's Famous logo with its cartoon penis hands. We'd gone to see the hot dog eating contest. This was before I went to St. Jude's, and we would just get high and do dumb shit. *Is that what my life would be like again?*

"In a way," said Max, passing what was left of the joint, "neither of us really needs *Gossip Girl* anymore. I was thinking of dipping even before this happened."

"I mean, I like working with you. Just trying to follow the money, you know."

"Of course."

"And you have your writing thing. Now you can do that full-time." *My writing thing.* "I mean, it's not like the site wasn't helpful for me. My back-end skills are fire now."

Max kept talking, but I wasn't really listening anymore. *Other than* Gossip Girl, *I hadn't written shit. For months now.*

S6E1: "Gone Maybe Gone"
Nate's POV

Where are we?

"Your unconscious mind."

Am I going to have to see, like. Fucked up things from my past.

"Is there anything in particular that you're avoiding?"

Aren't you the one who's supposed to tell me things like that?

"Why would I? I don't know why I'm here either."

What the fuck?

He still couldn't see anything.

Nate wanted to think, but he wasn't sure if Lauren Berlant could read his mind. *Who knew that the dead could be such a bitch.* When they were zapped back into the Plaza, he walked to the dresser and almost ripped it open, balled up socks spilling onto the floor. He found the emergency Backwoods wrapper, mango flavored, and the q of Monkey's Breath.

What does it feel like to smoke weed when you're already dead?

"God, I don't know why I stopped smoking weed when I was alive. I'm such a fucking idiot."

He didn't know what to say to Lauren after that. He didn't know any philosophy. He asked them if they wanted to watch some hotel TV and they said sure.

Here. He tossed the remote to Lauren. *You choose.*

Lauren flipped past an ad for a panini machine, updates on civilian casualties in Afghanistan, the Dow plummeting, suicidal, and eventually picked *Eternal Sunshine of the Spotless Mind* (2004). Outside, it was almost morning. The rain had turned to mist. As Lauren burned through a pack of sugar-free wintermint gum, they watched the famous scene, the one that appears on the poster: Kate Winslet and Jim Carrey, cast against type, lying on a frozen lake.

"Have you seen this movie before?

My ex-girlfriend Blair used to like it a lot.

"What did she like about it?"

"I don't know. I guess that it made her feel." In her 2021 *e-flux* essay, writer Maxi Wallenhorst described dissociation as a "veil."

Arriving three years before the official introduction of the term, Kate Winslet's character, Clementine, nonetheless exemplifies the manic pixie dream girl archetype. Jim Carrey plays Joel, the simultaneously repressed yet deeply feeling man whose life is literally brightened (Clementine's hair is dyed bright orange, clementine-colored) by a quirky, impulsive female protagonist. In a way, their dynamic is just an example of heteronormativity itself: her excess is both enabling and too much; his caution is both stabilizing and asphyxiating.

After a sudden break-up, Carrey shows up to the Barnes & Noble where Clementine works only to find that she doesn't recognize him. At first, he thinks it's a joke. Just the manic pixie dream girl being manic again. But when Clementine asks, "Can I help you, sir?" from behind the register before making out with Elijah Wood–hot off playing a hobbit in *Lord of the Rings* (2001-3)–Joel sees it's for real.

And of course it is: thanks to a company called Lacuna, Clementine has wiped Jim Carrey from her mind. Vengeful, hurt, and yet still mirroring addictively, Joel decides to visit Lacuna and delete Kate Winslet as well. "The nebbish man and the dream-woman both erase their memories," writes Lauren Berlant in *Desire/Love* (2012). The thing about being the chosen one is that it means you're chosen. When Nate turns around to ask Lauren for some gum, he finds that they are crying quietly. He isn't sure what to do–if this is the quiet, cathartic sobbing that people watch movies for in the first place, or if it's something else going on. Awkwardly, he gets up, goes to the bathroom, and comes out with a roll of toilet paper. Hands it to Lauren.

"I shouldn't be crying."

Why not? The movie is sad.

"It's not even the movie. It's just..." Onscreen, Jim Carrey walks through a beach house which is gradually flooding with ocean water. He apologizes to Clementine–not for being nasty to her, calling her an alcoholic, an attention-seeking slut, but for being afraid. But he isn't afraid of what he thinks he's afraid of. What he truly has to be sorry for, he doesn't even know he's done. *Maybe I shouldn't have asked that*, Nate thinks, wondering if Lauren had heard him think that. He unfurled another thin, beige rolling paper from the pack of Raws.

"I died before my last book was published," Lauren said. "I know I shouldn't care. It's just work, after all, and it feels like such a capitalist thing to obsess over now. Like, the world is falling apart and all I can think about is my job? What's wrong with me? But it was one of the only things I had." They looked away with what could have been bitterness or shame. "That wasn't how it should have been, but it's how it happened."

Joel keeps leaving Clementine. He loves and can't bear to be with her; because he loves her, she is unbearable. He has meltdowns. He yells at her. He kicks her out of his car, all the emotions he can't let himself feel coming out, horribly.

TIME OUT
December 17, 2015, 7:31 pm
Filed under: affect, ambivalence, Attachment, Craziness, flatness, Mood, sovereignty, supervalent_thought, teaching, Theory of this Blog, writing

For the last 24 hours I've been unscheduled. I had taken a gig in Amsterdam scheduled right after the term so I could interrupt my habits of working, working out, professing, sleeping a little & waking up, opening the window so that the cat could smell the world and then sitting down at the desk with my habitual combo of detox tea and coffee, because who am I if not balanced, before I extend myself to become unbalanced. The great thing about writing is that it is flat even when it's other things too.

I never take vacations, and days off are rare failures to be very off at all, as I narrate here yearly if I manage actually to try–it just occurs to me now that my drive to keep my infinitives unsplit (so that your verbs will be strong, I tell my students) has something to do with my drive to hold myself together too, as an action figure of a cool figuration otherwise than to be/not to be but feeling out attachment heuristically. With all this work, I am a slow reviser: I have been ahead of many curves, but now some curves are ahead of me and it doesn't matter, I hope, because a curve's curve requires lots of leaning one way by many people before it becomes a thing that's banking as a stability and not just a longing for solidity at the end of some road, like a home. Continue reading →

2 COMMENTS

Lauren Berlant. "Time Out." *Supervalent Thought* (December 17, 2015)

"I'm not a nice person, Nate," he heard Lauren say. "I could be cruel, competitive, difficult–all the traits I despised in others–it's because I saw them in myself. But with my work, it was the opposite. And this book especially..."

How come?

"I mean, it's stupid, but this was supposed to be my trans book, you know? Like this is was the one where I officially say–this is me. It's a trite gesture by now, of course. But still. I'd never really done it before. I was using they/them with my students before I died. And even before trans was a whole...thing or whatever, the commune I lived in when I was in high school, Twin Oaks, had a gender neutral pronoun: Co. And I used it for years. And got my ass handed to me in grad school for being pretentious. So stopped."

Damn. What the hell. That's so fucked.

"Bad timing, I guess." Lauren laughed.

At the end of movie, post-lobotomy Kate Winslet and Jim Carrey learn that they've had their memories erased. In the process of finding their minds, the two protagonists listen to the cassette tape (vintage!) recordings that each made of the other at Lacuna, outlining why they've chosen to erase the other from their minds. Kate says she wants to delete Joel because "he's boring. Is that enough of a reason?" *How happy is the blameless vestal's lot! The world forgetting, by the world forgot. Eternal sunshine of the spotless mind! Each pray'r accepted, and each wish resign'd.* Joel says Clementine tricks people into liking her by fucking them. It's bizarre, not only because Clementine never even flirts with (let alone sleeps with) another man, but because we never even see her sleep with Joel. They're in love, sure, but their love is sterile and twee. Thanks to being white, they aren't just child-like, but children already, hitting each other with bed pillows, frolicking in snow.

Despite learning everything they hate in each other, Kate Winslet and Jim Carrey decide to fall in love again. Or they don't choose: they're in love already. The problem isn't wanting bad objects. Or it is, but even before that, there's the problem of wanting at all. Wanting to want. But not being able to. Every fresh soda you open is somehow already flat.

Early Riser
Blair's POV

Mornings are the only time I feel like me. I've always been an early riser. Even with a late night and a hangover, I'm usually up by nine o'clock. I don't know. I can't help it. I drink my coffee with one lump of sugar and cream, which is not very low on fat, unless you count the coffee as breakfast. Then it's fine. Sometimes I set an alarm, and sometimes I'm convulsed by panic. Then I wake up. My mother is gone, Dorota is there with coffee and grapefruit. It's the perfect breakfast. The most transactional, the most perfect form of intimacy.

S5E5: "The Fasting and the Furious"
Gordon's POV

My flight to LA was delayed because of the fires. Then it was delayed again because of COVID. After a certain point, they just sent me home from the airport and booked me another flight, free, for two weeks down the road.

When I got there, Nia picked me up.

"What the actual fuck."

"Isn't this insane?" she said, pointing to her hot pink convertible. "It's modeled off Devan Aoki's *Fast and Furious* car."

"Did you buy it?"

"Lol. I wish. I'm promoting some app." She shrugged. We were driving down Sunset Boulevard. Some of the famous palm trees were charred. Nia's car glittered in the hazy polluted sun. *Exchange value and sex appeal. The only things that would last.*

The network had booked an Airbnb for everyone, but Nia said I could stay with her in Silver Lake.

"I always forgot that people in LA live in houses," I said, dropping my bag in the guest bedroom. "With like, multiple floors."

"New Yorkers love suffering."

She asked if I wanted to go out and I said no, I was tired from my flight, and besides we had to be up early for a stupid team meeting thing.

"Okay, thank God. I'm exhausted also. I'm supposed to do an event tonight but now I have an excuse to blow it off. Do you want me to order Thai?"

Ostensibly for work, but also because we were both shy, actually—those people who are always online because they're awkward and dumb IRL—we did some K, and started ambiently discussing surguries.

"My bottom surgeon is *sexy*. Like hot. That's why I trust him. And clearly he's had work done."

"He's transgender?"

"Of course not," said Nia. We both laughed. "But the aura is Ken doll. Like whoever makes him look plastic, I want that."

"My surgeon is some jock. Benjamin. *American Psycho* vibes. I don't even care."

"How many phallo guys are in New York?"

"I mean, some of the start-ups started offering it like a year ago–"

"Same in LA."

"Are they good here?"

"Maybe in four or five years..."

Onscreen, Tavi Gevinson was saying words about *The Paris Review*.

"It's cool that you're getting your thing done so young."

"Yeah."

"Not in any like..."

"You're so fine. And you're right. I'm very lucky."

I usually tried not to think about the age difference too much. As in, I thought about it all the time, trying to act like a cool older brother or chill uncle while also treating Nia as my peer, friend, and colleague, which she was. Going through trans stuff at the same time meant that while we were experiencing our second puberties simultaneously, I was almost in my mid-thirties, and she was–what? Twenty-five? I tried not to be bitter about the life she'd get to have, the one that had been impossible for me. I tried to be happy that, whatever real life was, someone was living it.

We finished eating, cleared the plates, took out the trash.

The Live-Action *Lion King* (2019)

Celebs now live a second life as the voice actors of CGI'd Disney cartoons. Fantasy is deathless. Only reality dies. In a capitalist realist twist, the deep state forbade DC, Marvel and Disney from making original content. After 2024. They just said, "This is it." The live action remake of *101 Dalmatians* was better than you might think. *Cruella* (2021)–featuring Emma Stone's best role–admits to the co-presence of beauty and cruelty.

But the live-action *Lion King* sucked. The cast was even more star-studded than usual, with Beyoncé as Nala and Seth Rogan as Pumbaa the adorable warthog. The digital imagery is perfect. It is what Hito Steyerl would call a "rich image," defined by high quality, peak resolution and sharpness. If you reached out and touched the screen, you would find, not a digital surface, but objects. "Obviously," Steyerl writes, "a high-resolution image looks more brilliant and impressive, more mimetic and magic, more scary and seductive than a poor one. It is more rich, so to speak."

The live-action *Lion King* (2019) was a rich image but had "no emotions," to quote Showbiz Cheat Sheet. The protagonists in the cartoon original was animated with human faces, anthropomorphized to give them legible feelings except, in the very last instance, when their status as fake images shielded them from death. Cartoons never died, but the live action animals emoted like animals. They felt–deeply, of course–but their emotions were scrawled on their faces, indecipherable.

Remakes don't have to be good. Franchises cash in on existing intellectual property (a farcical construction of immaterial capitalism itself) via existing material, converting old shows into content for streaming platforms. *Friends* on HBO and all that. But the franchise model is forward-looking as well, capitalizing on extant fan bases as guaranteed market sectors. The *Lion King* remake didn't have to be good because fans would watch anyway, if not for pleasure, than out of morbid curiosity. To quote Rodrigo Nunes, "Those who believed radical change was inevitable after 2008 ....did not foresee the extent to which our political systems have become inured to running on low legitimacy."

If it's not too clunky, we can think of the development and distribution of the live action *Lion King* as an allegory. Neoliberalism, positioning itself as an inevitable technocratic regime, tells us that it is endless, as common sense as cost benefit analysis. The endlessness of covid is likewise naturalized, as if the pandemic had to last this long, there was nothing we could do, even as each new wave is experienced, much like the live action *Lion King*, as an unsurprising surprise.

S5E7: "The Big Sleep No More"
Chuck's POV

After Dan left, I did what I always do after sex: go to the hotel I own, to the penthouse suite I own, lie down, watch the sun come up. People think of me as a connoisseur: of Grey Goose vodka, of married women who want to fuck sixteen year olds, of Gucci loafers. What they don't know is how much I love a sunrise. How many of them I've seen. All true nightlife people see the sun come up. If you're out late—well, there you are. Today the sun was nipple-colored. Creamy as shit.

The penthouse has the best bathtubs. That's another thing I love. Every room should have a bathtub if you think about it. This is why I'm so good at being me. I don't know what they put in the baths at Empire (that's the name of the hotel I own) but I just ask them to leave extra of it, all the little salts and sugars, like I'm my own chai latte. Whatever. I'm Chuck Bass.

That's how he got me—because I was in the bath. Nodding off. Totally safe. Just something I do sometimes. So I didn't hear him when he opened the door, shut it, sat at the table in a suit, on his Blackberry. Of course I didn't hear it. I was listening to "Kids" by MGMT on loop. He could have said something. Woken me up. Or I don't know. Told me that he was coming. Told me that he wasn't actually fucking dead. He could have not pretended to be fucking dead. "Whatever I do, you'll forgive me later." That's what he would always tell me after doing something unforgivable.

Isn't it funny that both of my parents faked their deaths? First my mother. Bart told me that I killed her. That she died in childbirth. Giving birth to me. Very reverse Oedipus. Because I'm a faggot. Kill the mother, fuck the father, etc. Important to take it all (life) extremely literally. Great way to make your son feel like shit forever, make him feel indebted to you forever, make him feel guilt on his back just for even existing, just lie and tell him, "You killed your mom." *You could have said some different shit, Bart. She could have been hit by a car while crossing the street and I was just too young to remember it. I wouldn't have exited the bath fully naked and itching my sudsy ballsack if I'd known that you'd be sitting there, Daddy, watching me.*

"What the fuck." *I thought I was hallucinating. Like fuck I knew I was fucked but I'd just done alcohol and some uppers, nothing insane, unless someone had fucked with me??* "You're dead."

"Well, clearly not."

"You're talking to me from the dead."

"Dead people don't talk, Chuck."

"Then why are you talking." *I looked at his glass.*

"Well, you're starting early."

"It's water. Not that you know what that is." *Fuck you.* I looked at him. Jeff Bezos himself. Usually I order up a pair of clean underwear but I wasn't going to do that with Bart around. I put on a robe.

"Okay, then. Do your bit."

"What do you mean."

"You know. The thing where explain why you faked your death and then don't apologize."

"I'd apologize if I thought what I'd done was wrong," said Bart/Jeff Bezos/my dad. "But I was just trying to help you Chuck. I know you don't see that now, but you will in fifteen to twenty years. Trust me."

"I don't trust you."

"But you will, Chuck. You'll be forced to. In fifteen to twenty years. When the world stops."

"Stops?" I laughed. "What are you going to do? Stop it?"

"It has nothing to do with me. Fifteen years is when we run out of water."

"But doesn't Bart Industries own reservoirs in Brazil, Russia, Canada and the United States?"

"It's not just drought. It's also the fires. They'll hit the midwest. The Lower East Side will start to flood. Food supply chains all fucked. Your downtown girls? Your Blair Waldorf? They'll be eating slugs on toast." I laughed again. I couldn't help it.

"Blair? Whose favorite foods are wagyu and caviar?"

"She'll be lucky to be eating slugs," Bart said. "Listen, Chuck. I want you to picture it."

"Get the fuck out of my head."

"Chuck. I'm saying this because I care. I want you to picture this. Imagine your girlfriend–Blair–with her nice brown and her pretty skin–and imagine her opening up a sardine tin except instead of sardines, it's slugs. And then I want you to imagine her putting those slugs on toast and biting."

"You've outdone yourself," I told him. "Truly, this villain monologue is better than anything I might have expected. You do the exposition thing, you try to make us see your side, and we even get a little moment of gross out humor, as a treat."

"Biting and chewing slugs. And feeling happy. Because it's better than not having food." Then he said one of the things that he loved to say. *So in character, Bart. Just you being you.* "Please don't disappoint me, Chuck. Even more than you already have." *He was making me miss the sunrise. It was almost morning now. Real morning. When the sky is blue and other people go to work.*

"I've been in outer space," Bart continued. He was always continuing because his talking never stopped. "Preparing. For when the world stops. So that, when it does, we have a place to go. You, me, and a few other people. Elon Musk, of course. Zuckerberg, that weird little shit."

"So what, all the rich villains are getting sucked up to Mars?"

"The moon."

"Fuck." I put my head in my hands. *Fuck Fuck fuck fuck fuck.*

"Charles."

"You're a reptile."

I looked out the window. It was raining now. *Right on fucking cue.* Drizzle through the headlights. Glittery puddles on the streets. *All that cliche New York shit. It would all be gone.*

"Chuck. I pretended to be dead because what I was working on had to be secret. Even from you. And I'm sorry for the harm that caused. But I did what I did too protect you. And you will be protected now. We have somewhere to go. You can even bring Blair."

"Blair can come?" *I was embarrassed to hear my voice crack. Who was I, a fucking faggot. In front of my dad.*

"I–I'll talk to her." Bart laughed. His laugh always freaked me out. Because it didn't sound how you'd expect a villain to sound. He laughed like a child. Like the happiest kid in the world. *Which, most likely, he was.*

Period Piece

Gregg Araki makes period pieces. If the *Teenage Apocalypse Trilogy* gave us nineties post-AIDS grunge-core, *Kaboom* (2010) gives us "the Recession just happened" aughts: neon and black, animal masks, straight boys in tank tops, post-Scene hair, partying, wanting to die, American Apparel hoodie. Vibes are the bleak-as-fuck EDM opener to Katy Perry's "Firework," first released in 2010: "Do you ever feel like a plastic bag / Drifting through the wind, wanting to start again?" In a 2014 essay that also touched on Perry as well as the comparatively crazed "I Gotta Feeling" by the Black Eyed Peas, critic Mark Fisher wrote, "It's hard not to hear these records' demands that we enjoy ourselves as thin attempts to distract from a depression that they can only mask, never dissipate.... Partying is a job in another sense—in conditions of objective immiseration and economic downturn, making up the affective deficit is outsourced to us."

Smith, the protagonist, parties. Smith goes hard. Smith has been having weird dreams. Ray-bans, necklaces, purple cotton cardigan. Smith gets a note underneath his door, not even hand-written, but with the words "YOU ARE THE CHOSEN SON" imprinted in red helvetica, looking like something you'd buy at a twee bookstore beneath a finger mustache mug.

S5E15: "Crazy Cupid Love"
Nate's POV

When it was morning again, I asked Lauren if they wanted me to order room service, but they said they weren't hungry. We got coffee. I drank my cappuccino as Lauren sipped their genmaicha green tea. When I finished my croissant, I noticed, almost by accident, that my body was normal again. I looked at both sides of my hands. Then went to the mirror: my face.

Is it permanent?

"I don't know." *Would I ever know?* I brushed the surfaces of my arms, legs, stomach, all newly taut with skin.

God. I'm just–I'm so sick of being in this room.

Twenty minutes later, we were at the Upper East Side Pinkberry eating frozen yogurt.

I know it's like, a girly thing, but god. I fucking love this stuff.

"What toppings did you get?"

Strawberry, blackberry, and mochi, which are, um, gummy bears made of rice. Lauren ordered mango mochi, and coconut. I wondered how the cashier could see ghosts. Lauren said that of all the frozen yogurt chains, Pinkberry had always been their favorite because of the tartness. *I didn't know that the undead ate froyo.* Lauren shrugged. A small fleck of coconut hung on their lower lip before detaching itself and falling, noiselessly, onto the street.

"Thanks for being such a sweetheart last night, by the way."

What? I just smoked you out.

"I was sent here to help you, and…I don't know. Just ended up talking about my own shit."

It's fine. Don't beat yourself up.

The thing about Pinkberry is you have to plan it, making sure to eat the toppings and froyo at a fairly even rate. Otherwise, you're just left with a weird cup of fruit.

It's nice to be reminded that I can. Be there for people I care about.

Suddenly, I woke up.

S5E18: Con Heir
Gordon's POV

When we came back in, it was late. Our first meeting was tomorrow. Nine thirty. "I don't get why it's that early. It literally doesn't have to be."

"At least it's not in person."

"Marcus has big 'I wake up early' vibes."

"Ugh. I'm going to sleep," said Nia. "Before I get annoyed. Do you need anything?"

"Advil? I fucked up my leg going running today. Or, I don't know. It's like a consistent thing. My right quad."

"Oh sure. There's also ice in the freezer. Do you want to use my massage gun?"

"You have everything."

"I can't help it," she said, walking into another room. "I'm a fucking PREPPER."

Nia's massage gun kind of looked like a cross between a vibrator and a glock. "It actually starts recharging itself as soon as you turn it off."

"Cool." She turned it on for me and watched as I applied it, wincing, to my left and then right quad. "Is it helping?"

"Yeah." Then she said something else, but I couldn't hear it. The massage gun was too loud.

"You aren't a creep is what I said."

I turned the massage gun off, startled. "Wait–I'm so sorry. Was I…"

"No. That's what I mean."

"Oh. Okay." I thought I'd been normal but now it just felt like I'd fucked up.

"Don't worry," she said, and smiled. "I don't have a crush on you."

"Well, I don't have a crush on you. I mean, you're hot–"

"I know."

"And like. A beautiful famous micro-celebrity."

"I just wish I were rich."

I hadn't had a crush on Nia. It hadn't even occurred to me to do that. And yet–maybe only because she'd brought it up–I suddenly wanted to imagine that she *could* have a crush on me. That it was technically possible. Not a crush I'd want her to act on. I just wanted her to think I was hot. I remembered once, years ago, dysphoric during sex, I did a thing that sometimes happened to me–stopped fucking, pulled out, lay there, non-verbal, humiliated. It wasn't a one-off but it was a girl from the apps. Even then, we couldn't remember each other's names. She was trans also, and sweet. I apologized for not being able to make her cum, ordered a cab, and left.

S5E24: "The Return of the Ring"
Dan's POV

The first few days were quiet. I don't know what I was expecting, or what I wanted. I couldn't even compose the last post. I didn't give an explanation. Just asked Max to bang out some PR language saying *Gossip Girl* was shutting down, told him not to even give a reason, just say it was "time."

I saw Serena a few hours after the post went up.

"Hey."

It was lunch. She'd asked me to meet somewhere private. We were in Central Park walking around the Great Lawn, watching the skyline dip in and out of view.

"What happened to you that day? You never showed up. And then I see on *Gossip Girl* that you're with Nate and there are all these rumors–"

"Dan, you know how *Gossip Girl* is. She'll say anything for clicks."

"That's not the point." *I knew I was being a dick. So why couldn't I stop myself.*

"I'm not cheating on you with Nate. I know he and I have a history, but he's going through it right now. And he needed to talk to me. That's all." *I wanted to say something hurtful. I could feel it. And how easy it would be. To tell Serena that I didn't believe her. To tell her I believed her, but she could have called, she didn't have to leave me stranded, that this was just proof that she didn't care and in fact she never did, she never had, she was always, always abandoning me. Even when we were together. Even right now.*

Don't do it, Dan. Don't self-sabotage.

"Okay. I believe you," I said.

"You do?" *The phrase that first came to my mind was that "Serena breathed a sigh of relief," but that is in fact what happened. Sometimes the stock image phrase is true.* "Thank you, Dan."

"You don't have to thank me for trusting you." T*he demons in my head were screaming. Say something normal.* "Is Nate okay?"

"I don't know. We met up at the Plaza obviously. And then he told me this thing that was fully insane–that he'd been put on some kind of trans pills that physically turned him into his father?"

"What?'

"I think he's having some kind of breakdown." It would be summer soon. St. Jude's boys, uniform shirts unbuttoned, ties undone, were playing frisbee on the Great Lawn. Some German tourists, all wearing matching floral rompers, ate Magnolia Bakery cupcakes on the grass.

"Have you talked to him since then?"

"He said he was getting a room at the Plaza. And now he won't return my messages or calls." *In a past life, this news about Nate's breakdown would have been a hot* Gossip Girl *tip. And now it was just... nothing. It was just a fact.*

"Jesus."

"Yeah."

"Well, I'm glad that you could be there for your friend."

"Me, too. And–I'm sorry that I didn't tell you about it sooner. I'm not always good with sharing what's going on with me. I get so scared of letting you down."

"The truth is scary. I get scared, too." *You lied to Serena more than she ever lied to you.*

"Really?"

"Of course. This is just communication. Totally normal couples stuff."

Serena bit her lip and then she kissed me. She held my face in her hands and she kissed my face. I kissed her back. I put my hand on the back of her neck and pushed her closer to me.

"I love you."

"I love you, too."

"I love you so, so much."

I could never tell her. I could never tell her any of it.

We went to a part of the park that was empty and fucked. I thought of rich cyclists zipping by and catching blurry glimpses of our bodies. I wondered if they would stop and look at us. If anyone would. I came as I choked Serena and she came from watching me cum.

New Rules

Sometimes people are sick in the head for the exact same reason but it manifests in such opposite ways that when they meet up, instead of bonding, they cringe at each other, in agony.

Dua Lipa was never that good at social cues. When she was a teenager, this confused people. Clearly she was hot but also something was Off. She was hitting all the steps but dancing to the wrong track, and no one would tell her except by their faces, which looked uncomfortable and confused.

So Dua Lipa, who was nothing if not a hard worker, decided to obsessively learn every social cue ever. It was like going to a coding boot camp except for learning how to interact. *I got new rules; I count 'em*, she would think to herself as she Wiki'd "autism special interest."

Charli XCX was never that good at social cues. She was hot, though, and confident—maybe it was being white-passing, maybe it was performing in London warehouse clubs by the time she was 14. She knew something was Off, but if she could just get to do the things she was good at, the rest would sort itself out. When she didn't know what was going on, when people's words felt like water going down the drain, she anxiously tried to improv it. *I feel so unstable, fucking hate these people / How they're making me feel lately.*

Dua Lipa and Charli XCX performed together sometimes, were often grouped together due to being two ethnically ambiguous brunettes who made hyper-pop adjacent tracks. But there's a reason you never see Dua Lipa cameo on a Charli XCX album, and it's because they made each other fucking insane. When Dua saw Charli talk at Kim Petras then fake grind Troye Sivan at the 2019 VMA after party, she wanted to scream. *I learned the rules. I fucking worked to learn the new rules. And you just...think you don't have to? You think you deserve to just get in for free?*

Charli knew that she pissed Dua off. She just didn't know why. She saw the bitch give her looks at the VMAs and it's like *oi bro why are you always mad at me? If you've got an issue ya, just tell me? Instead of trying to passive aggressively manage my vibes? It's not like I don't want to be your friend, it's just—why the fuck do you make it so hard?*

They both left the 2019 VMAs early. Went home. Scrolled for a bit. Went to bed alone.

S6E3: "Dirty Rotten Scandals"

Blair's POV

"You don't miss her?"

"Who, *Gossip Girl*? Of course not." We were sitting on the Met steps.

"You don't miss being the star of the show?"

"Blair, believe it or not, appearing on *Gossip Girl* wasn't exactly my idea of fun." *But she made you, Serena. She made you who you are. Now you're an actor without a set.*

"I mean, you must have enjoyed it a little bit. Who doesn't love the spotlight? Especially when that someone is you." Serena looked at me. "Blair?"

"What?"

"Do I always make you this unhappy?"

The Most Dangerous Philosopher in the West

In 2015, *Vice* interviewed Slavoj Zizek. On YouTube, the piece is called "Superstar Communist Slavoj Zizek is the Most Dangerous Philosopher in the West."

The interviewer is welcomed into Zizek's Ljubljana home: overstuffed floral sofa, a portrait of Stalin in the front hallway which is there "just to annoy people," Zizek explains. "I'm the Joker from Batman." He sniffs and talks like someone on coke. Whether or not he's on coke, he wants to look like he's on coke. "I may be the Joker from Batman, but I can be Stalin. If you give me power, I know how to use it."

Zizek's comments reject close readings; they slide off his Teflon-coated words. If you are alarmed by the Stalin comparison, then you're the loser, the one who doesn't get genre: you've taken the joke too seriously. Yet claiming to not be saying anything at all can be a way to say something very specific, something which cannot be said explicitly because it's contents are fascistic. Nonsense launders meaning; that's why it's there.

In a 2017 piece for *The New Inquiry*, Lauren Berlant argues that the jokester and the predator operate by creating moments of "improvisatory boundary-drawing." The two figures are thus linked, moving in similar ways, but for ostensibly different ends: "Where the predator creates a situation they can exploit, it is often cushioned by a menacing sense that they control the interactive space and that they're unavoidable. When a goof performs a joke, which is mostly spontaneous and casual, it is shaped by the play of surprise and hard to process in the moment. Time and fresh awkwardness provide the jokester's cushion, however slight." Sometimes it is hard to tell the jokester and predator apart. Sometimes, someone is both; for Berlant, this both-ness was exemplified by both the Me Too movement and the Trump presidency. Engaging with someone who is both the Joker and Stalin might leave you suddenly feeling "baffled or overwhelmed."

Reading literally allows us to see that people like Zizek do in fact mean what they say. While Zizek never morphed into a fully Stalinist tankie LARP, his bigotry became more explicit as the 2010s came to a close.

Trans people, he argued, were a confused product of PC culture, birthed in the twenty-first century from a verve for both categorization and fluidity in addition to a chronic need to feel special. Instead of rejecting the neoliberalization of identity–which drives towards individuation instead of collectivity–peopled transitioned because they wanted an identity, thereby socially reproducing capitalist logic at everyone else's expense.

As a brief comparison, we can contrast Zizek thoughts on specialness with Berlant's comments on similar topics from a 2019 interview:

"I just watched Won't You Be My Neighbor?*, a film about Fred Rogers and his children's show* Mr. Rogers' Neighborhood. *At one point the film splices in broadcasts of right-wing rage at Rogers's insistence that each child is special and deserves the comfort of explanation about what's overwhelming about life, even at the smallest scales. The right keeps saying that people should have to fight for their specialness, should have to earn being valued and valuable.... Under authoritarian and supremacist regimes one is supposed to earn the right to exist rather than to be respected and cultivated because they exist."*

To quote Ariana Grande, "Imagine a world like that."

S6E8: "It's Really Complicated"
Gordon's POV

The meeting was whatever. I don't even remember it. I spent forever prepping for some shit that my brain just put on auto-delete. Why the fuck do I even try.

We got In-N-Out and ate it by the water.

Then Nia had to go do a thing with a rich person. "Which you can come to if you want. But I think you'd be bored. I mean. I will be bored. So."

"Will you actually?" She laughed in a way that I couldn't interpret.

"I'll find some way to entertain myself. And have fun. I mean, that's my job."

"Literally so true."

"What are you going to do tonight?"

"I don't know. Just chill? Prepare for tomorrow. Ugh."

"I know. Stupid."

"I know. I need to like–brainwash myself to be into it. Otherwise I'll just keep fucking up."

I thought I would get work done while Nia was out but I couldn't focus so instead I just cleaned the house. Not that it wasn't clean already, but if you want to clean manically and not think about anything then there's always something for you to do of course. Like take out the trash and recycling, vacuum, wash the tub. I thought Nia would be out late but she wasn't. When she came in, I was listening to a podcast and scrubbing the fridge, didn't even hear her car pull up.

"–you?"

"What?" She put her bag down. "I can't believe you cleaned. That's so sweet."

"I just needed something to do. How was your thing? Do you want a joint?" I'd thought the weed in California would be be better but Nia told me that what with the fires and weed being fully legal in New York for a years now, it was basically the same. *New York and LA are finally the same now.* Time reached out and flattened itself.

Nia didn't want to talk about the event, so we smoked and watched *Gossip Girl* wordlessly on her flatscreen TV. "I'm sorry if what I said was weird," she said after a while. "About the crush thing."

"It wasn't weird."

"Are you sure."

"Yeah. Clarifying boundaries is normal and good. And besides. We have the same boundaries. So there's not even a conflict."

"Okay." Onscreen, Nate said words emphatically, a bug preserved in amber. His perfect hair crinkled with light.

"The other thing I forgot to say is that I'm a lesbian."

'What?"

"I'm a lesbian." It was a different episode now. Nate went jogging in Central Park.

"You're a lesbian? Same."

"Shut up!" *That weirdly does make it better somehow.* Nia cracked ice from the ice tray into two glasses that looked like cubes. Grabbed coconut water from the fridge. "Ugh. Don't trans boys know that their constant crisis of masculinity is the most cisgender thing about them? Did we finish that joint?"

The next two meetings were weirdly better and then I flew back to New York.

S5E20: “Salon of the Dead”
Nate’s POV

When I checked out of the Plaza, they told me that I’d been there a week. I paid the bill with my mom’s card and then called Serena, who said I could stay with her. I just remember lying down in the guest bedroom and when I woke up it was the weekend.

“Where’s Lauren?”

“Oh my god. Nate.”

“Serena. Hi.”

“Do you want some, like, water?”

“Thank you.” I sat up. The AC was on. It made a faint, blurry sound. The glass Serena gave me was mostly ice.

“Are you okay? I honestly didn’t know if you were on some like weird drugs or what so I called a doctor but he said you just had a fever and to let you sleep. Actually,” she looked at her phone. “I’m supposed to text him. Let him know you’re up. God, I’m so glad you’re alright. Who’s Lauren, by the way?”

Prepwear Returns

2021 Fall Fashion week just looked like *Gossip Girl*. Not even the reboot but the original: ties (on girls and boys), pleated skirts, hyper-tailored pants in prints like houndstooth and plaid. Prep aesthetics had trickled down into fast fashion, too. Uniqlo sold sweater vests as part of their "back to school" collection, while, around town ("street style" we were told, was "back") everyone's uniform included loafers, to be worn with or without socks. There was the Gucci kind (with horsebit buckles); there was the Telfar kind (with the circular Telfar logo where a buckle might otherwise be).

There are ways to read this that aren't wrong just because they're obvious. It's a rejection of quarantine athleisure. The return of prep school aesthetics both channels a desire to go "back to school" (work, life, "normal") in a world where actually doing so doesn't maybe mean death. New York Fashion week almost collided head-first with NYC's public schools "reopening" for the first time in eighteen months; unvaccinated children in their ties, sweater vests pleated skirts; models in their ties, sweater vests, pleated skirts.

There are ways to read this that aren't wrong just because they're less obvious. Professional trend forecaster Ayesha Siddiqi argues that "as more and more traditional structures are destabilized, less accessible, and grow to signify a total fantasy rather than an aspiration (as is typical of fashion), the uniforms and costumes of those settings will be clung to like remnants of a long gone more civilized civilization." Have we de-centered the present by acknowledging that the past Exists, or have we just leapt to replicate it, capitalist realism style? Repetition is glamorous. We all already know what you mean. You don't even have to try.

Fascists love a return to the past. Not just because it's the very definition of conservatism–instead of trying something new, we "conserve" the existing hegemonic norms–but because it's glamorous (you don't even have to try). Bondage-wear is so over, so woke era. And yet the Gucci horsebit buckles smuggle BDSM aesthetics into fall formal; whose turn is it to glamorize restraint? In "Notes on Deconstructing the Popular," Stuart Hall dissuades us from analyzing culture as a list of static objects and qualities. The point isn't what's on the market list, but how those objects are being utilized by power, upcycled and vomited out through the entertainment apparatus:

“Popular forms become enhanced in cultural value, go up the cultural escalator, find themselves on the opposite side. Other things cease to have high cultural value, and are appropriated back into the popular, becoming transformed in the process. The structuring principle does not consist of the contents of each category. Rather, it consists of the force and relations which sustain... the difference: roughly, between what, at any time, counts as an elite cultural activity or form, and what does not.”

“This season is about having fun again,” said Donatella Versace in a *Vogue* interview about her 2022 resort collection. Resort-wear is all about fun; it's what you wear to go on holiday. Of course, Versace's decision to give its prep take via resortwear makes the class connotations of prep-ware more obvious. Who goes to resorts (the rich). Who goes on vacations (the rich). We dress how we want to be (rich).

The fascists aren't wrong; the problem is that they are half right. The world is, in fact, ending. Or this world is. The spaceship to Mars will blast off soon and tickets are expensive. The earth is burning up, and condos on Elon Musk and Grimes's lunar villas are very pricey, despite their tacky eugenics-core aesthetic (each building looks like a sword). The fascists know the world is ending, but instead of doing something about it, they want to be where power is. They side with Jeff Bezos; when you try to get on the spaceship with your children, they execute you, stomping your child's skull and crushing it with the heels of their Gucci loafers, the horsebit buckles jingling.

My friend told me about a Tik Tok she watched “about the Kardashians, and about how the relatable or achievable aesthetics of the Kardashians are a way for people who cannot access their level of wealth to feel less class animosity toward them.” Of course, school uniforms have always been about punishment, part of the larger disciplinary apparatus of public and charter schools. Versace's resort menswear looks are fantastic. Matching tie and jacket, pattern printed with the gold chain Claudia Schiffer wore on her nineties Versace mini skirts; the Versace Medusa on a sweater vest, in lilac and black, under a black plaid suit. I would execute someone to wear them all.

I'm Chuck Bass
Chuck's POV

Chuck was a Sufjan Stevens fan. Had been since 2005 and *Illinois*.

Just one of the many secrets locked inside my heart.

He booked tickets for the girls as a clout move. To prove he was a baller who could. When Blair asked how he had access to the newest, dreamiest, Sufjan tracks before they even hit iTunes, he did what he always did. Shrug. Say, "I'm Chuck Bass."

But what did this mean? If you think about it? This tautological vibe? *I am myself. Is anyone?* He stepped into the jacuzzi tide pool and closed his eyes, letting the whirling jets shoot water up and his prostate and shaft.

"I'd give my body to be back again
In the rest of the room

To be alone with you
To be alone with you
To be alone with you."

One million little bubbles felt good on his ass. He imagined the future: outer space. No Nate ever again. With gentle, sociopathic precision, he drew the force field around his heart.

S4E1: "Belles Du Jour"
Vanessa's POV

We saw *Le Rayon Vert* (1986) at Film Forum and then walked west, to the water, to watch the New Jersey skyline twinkle in the night.

The break-up was so mutual that I can't even remember who suggested it.

"I was worried you'd think—I don't know. That I was just leaving because you were having a difficult time."

"Oh my god, Vanessa. No, not at all."

The vibes were off. They had been for a long time." *We had nothing in common. We never had. I'd known that even before the stuff with his dad. I'd find myself spending hours online, talking about Kiarostami movies with film nerds in other states. And then I'd see Nate and he'd ask me what I'd done all day and I wouldn't be able to tell him. Or I'd tell him, and he wouldn't know what to say. He'd just nod and be happy for me. He'd say that it sounded chill.*

Nate took a sip of Dragon Fruit Vitaminwater(™). "Damn. This tastes like shit."

"They all do."

We looked at pictures of dragon fruits on our flip phones. Looked at the Wiki, which explained that they grow on cactuses. Compared regular dragon fruits to the red ones, which look like red hand grenades and then, on the inside, are red also. *I'd worried that maybe I'd been cheating on Nate and not even realized it. Like, maybe I don't tell him about the forums because I have a crush on one of the guys and I'm having, like–an emotional romance. After a while, though, I realized that what I felt was less specific to any one person and more specific to the vibe. Which was happiness.*

"You seem good though."

"Me?" Nate laughed. "I don't know. Everyone thinks I'm insane."

"You seem more at peace."

"It's true," he said. "Are you?"

"Am I what? At peace?"

"Yeah."

I took another sip of diluted dragon fruit water. "I don't know what being at peace with myself would mean." *I'm going to leave Rufus's gallery/coffee shop. I'm going to quit my stupid job.*

"What?" said Nate.

"No, it's cliche."

"So is everything."

"Come on."

"No, I'm serious. Every cliche is fake and true."

The Hunger Games (the Lore)

Katniss Everdeen could be a fascist but also she could be a communist. Katniss Everdeen is whatever you need. That's why she's everyone's girl.The first time Gavin McGinniss watched *The Hunger Games: Mockingjay: Part One* (2014), he masturbated and cried, rewinding and rewatching the parts where Katniss shoots down an Imperial space ship with an explosive arrow. *Why aren't girls like that anymore*? When he founded the Proud Boys in 2016, Gavin McGinnis felt that Katniss would have joined them. At least, according to the lore. *The Capital is faggots anyway. Faggots and degenerate transsexual whores. It's giving the Weimar Republic. It's giving big end of empire vibes.*

Charli XCX could be a fascist but also she could be a communist. Charli XCX is whatever you need. That's why she's everyone's racially ambiguous white-passing girl. For the last six thousand years, conspiracy theorists have claimed that Charli XCX and Dua Lipa are in fact the same girl, produced by an algorithm which beamed their genetic material into two petri dishes, flowering simultaneously under the same fluorescent light. In fact, Charli XCX and Dua Lipa are not the same girl (according to the lore [Wikipedia]). Charli XCX and Dua Lia are different girls. Okay, they're both British. Okay, they both have brown hair. Okay, they're both hyper pop adjacent but also like, mainstream. In "Archiving the 20teens," Professional Trend Forecaster Ayesha Siddiqi argues that "emaciated Eastern Bloc models provide the fantasy not just of a white working class, but one whose alterity is vaguely ethnic, who look like the future we were told we escaped by trusting America's vision for the world." (Dua Lipa is Armenian. Charli is not). The way I avoided the cringe of id-pol was via the fantasy that I didn't have an identity at all.

And in a way, I don't, and it's fine, you're fine. I mean, you're doing what everyone does. I don't want to talk about it with you; you won't understand. Everything you know about me isn't fake per se but it's self-consciously stylized. I want you to know that I hide my real self from you. Charli XCX is just a fun and wacky girl. The interiority that she hides from us could be fascist or communist. It's good marketing, tap into multiple audience vectors. They can still hate each other and stan Charli XCX. This is not a poptimistic paragraph. For the "Good

Ones" music video, Charli asked the production team to generate a fake grave. Big gray tombstone that reads "Charli XCX."

Epilogue

S3E3: "The Lost Boy"
Nate's POV

It was a whatever day. *That's fine.* It was summer. High school was over. Just like that. Things exist, and then they don't. That happens sometimes. And–unless it's not–that's okay.

He'd quit the lacrosse team. That was good. In fact, he'd quit playing lacrosse entirely, turning down the lacrosse scholarship (not that he needed one) at Yale to study film at Columbia. Everyone had been shocked.

"It's not that I think you're stupid, Archibald," said Chuck. "Well, actually it is that."

"I know."

"You know what."

"That I'm dumb." He shrugged. "Never said I wasn't."

"So then why not be Yalie?" Chuck laughed. "Join Skull and Bones. Meet George Bush. Get some sweet consulting gig at McKinsey. Cruise control."

"Coasting," said Nate. "Right. I know. I will. Just at Columbia."

"They're the same, Nate."

"If they're the same, then why does it matter?"

"Because," said Chuck. "One is Yale."

It was like the Recession had never happened to Chuck. And it hadn't, in a way. His life was mostly the same. While my dad was in jail and then–missing from it. I didn't know how to feel. Well, I hated him of course. Not just impersonally, because he was my father, but personally, in the sense that all hatred is personal and impersonal; in the sense that my father was Bernie Madoff, and he had ruined the Archibald family. Chuck's father, the Bezos-coded logistics king, had benefited from the financial crash.

I realized in that moment that I hated my best friend.

"Hey," I said, pulling out my new cell (this thing called iPhone!) and checking the time. "I have to hop on a call."

"Business or pleasure?"

"Business, actually. For that summer internship thing."

"Archibald!" He smiled in that way which was almost a sneer. "Who's it with?"

"Probably. Some friend of Lily's. He's from LA. His name is Netflix. Kevin Netflix. They do. DVD rentals."

The internship thing was true, but there was no call. Just an hour to kill before I was meeting my mom for dinner at Nobu. She was depressed but off benzos now. I popped into a European looking cafe named after pain. *Le Pain Quotidien*. Pain is quotidien. *Yes*. I figured I'd get a cappuccino, wake up a bit, sit. I went to a log-shaped table made of wood at the center of the room shared by many different people I didn't know. And that's when I saw them. Eating a French-looking quinoa bowl and drinking espresso with a kind of gay guy, who also, weirdly, was eating a French-looking quinoa bowl and drinking...a turmeric latte?

No.

How is it possible.

Lauren Berlant.

How can-

But-

You're dead.

What do you do when that happens?

Do I tell them how dead they are?

Another option: I'm once again going fully insane.

That's when the second insane thing happened: Serena walked through Pain's door.

"Serena!" She turned instantly.

"Nate?"

"Hi." My voice sounded ragged. Deranged.

"Hey." I I waited for her to tell me how weird I looked, but she didn't even notice. She was too upset. Her mascara was running onto her button down shirt.

"Oh my god, Serena. Is everything okay?" She shook her head. "What's up?"

"I just...I don't know. It's me and Dan."

"Hey. Hey. It's okay. Let's get out of here. " I'm just going to run to the bathroom. I'll meet you outside." I waited for Serena to leave before picking up my iPhone and *New Yorker* tote and walking to where Lauren and the gay were talking.

"Lauren," I said. "Hey."

"Nate!" *So they knew me!!!*

"Lauren??? What are you doing here?"

"Well! Same to you!" *I thought you were dead.*

"Oh. Well." I blushed. "I was just...drinking coffee." Lauren looked neither surprised nor confused to see me. But they didn't look excited either.

"Well. I don't want to disrupt you if you're in the middle of something, but–I'd love to catch up sometime if you're free. I can give you my iPhone number."

"Wow. An iPhone." *What the fuck is going on here? It being a dream was one thing. But if it was real–and it meant nothing to them–?*

I reached into my tote and shuffled around until I found, *yes, thank God*, a pen. I scanned the gay; assigned him, reluctantly, an eight in my head. He looked American Apparel but grad school. I went back, grabbed a piece of my receipt, and scribbled my number on the back.

"Who was that?" said Serena as I stepped outside.

When I hugged her, I realized that I was crying. I hadn't cried in front of someone else in so long.

Premier
Gordon's POV

I didn't see Nia in person again for almost a year. We were supposed to both be on set, but COVID was so bad that even getting the actors and a skeleton crew was difficult enough. The first premier was in LA so that guests could still meet outside in February.

In a shocking plot twist (at least, to me personally) *Gossip Girl Three: the Gossip Games* was declared, not just a popular hit, but a critical success as well. By the time they announced the second premier in New York, timed to match the release of episode three, the show had already been greenlit for season two. Effie was upstate for the weekend with her boyfriend, so Nia stayed in her empty room.

I hated premieres but Nia thought they were funny so we smoked and then went together. "Just pretend it's part of your job," she said. "Customer service. Plus you get to see all these famous people act dumb." We got K'd out in the bathroom, so when Nia got pulled away to talk with Mary-Kate Olsen, it was honestly fine. Being at a premier was like being at home, in a way: do drugs, look at your phone. As long as you looked busy, it was fine to be alone.

"Gordon? What are you doing all alone here?" I looked up. *Marcus.* He looked goofy as ever—he was wearing some kind of newsboy cap?—but it didn't bother me anymore. It was just like, okay.

"I'm not alone. I'm with Nia. She just had to talk with an Olsen twin." Marcus laughed.

"May I?" He gestured to the chair next to me. When I sat down, I could tell that he was wasted. Other than coke, Marcus didn't really do drugs, which always felt so vintage. I waved at one of the bow-tied waiters and asked for two glasses of water. When it came—with a sprig of rosemary?—we finished our glasses in a single go, and Marcus clapped his hand around my shoulders, indicating brotherhood. "Proud of you, king."

"What for? You're the showrunner. If anything, I should be proud of you."

"We can be proud of each other," he said diplomatically, staring out into the crowd. Kristen Stewart and Cara Delavigne were laughing at something on one of their phones. "You excited for season two?"

"Totally."

"And guess what. I didn't tell you this yet, but they're giving us all a bonus."

"Holy shit. How much?"

"Fifty bars each. For getting a season two."

"Damn."

"I mean, it was in the contract."

"Yeah. Right."

"Plus double the salary for the next round. One hundred bars." I did the mental math without even trying. 100k plus 50k, plus 15k leftover from the last check. It was more money than I'd ever expected to make in my life. *That's like...what my mom makes. In a year.* "Financial stability," said Marcus, slapping my back again. "Just don't fuck it up this time. I can't afford it."

Someone in a muumuu announced that food was about to be served. Dinner was tuna tartare with garlic aioli served in a perfect square. Nia, back from her Olsen rendezvous, took a minuscule bite.

"It's Like a Rubik's Cube made of fish."

"Damn," said Marcus. "Better than the wedding reception ass food they had last year." He looked at Nia, chewing. "So bro. What does Gordy think of your new show? Sweet as fuck, huh?" He was glowing. He looked like someone's dad.

"What do you mean?" I said. "Like season two?"

"Fuck season two," Marcus said. "I mean, that's our bread and butter. But Nia's gonna have her own show, man. You didn't know?"

+

I was going to just take the train home, since the venue was near the F, but then Nia saw me heading out and said we should split a cab.

"Look," she said, pointing at her phone. "I already called it. Two minutes always." We sat there, saying nothing, the Uber ascending the bridge, twinkly skyline nights. Criterion Collection dot com. The radio was playing Charli XCX. *I wish I were smoking weed.*

"I was going to tell you," Nia said.

"It's fine."

"I just didn't want to tell you before it was confirmed. I didn't want to tell anyone."

"Marcus knew."

"Yeah, because this whole thing was his idea." She laughed. "Did you really think I didn't want you to know?"

"Nia, it's fine."

"I mean, it's clearly not."

"I just thought it was weird, because we talk, like. Everyday. But you don't have to tell me things just because I want you to. I mean, I'd feel bad if you didn't trust me or care or whatever. But other than that, it's just whatever is best for you."

"That's very parental."

"Don't call me that," I said, aware, suddenly, of the frantic edge in my voice. Nia frowned.

"What? I'm not like, saying you're old. I'm trying to give you a compliment."

"It's not about being old. It's just like..." I couldn't look at her. I looked back at the shimmering shot on film vibes view. "I have nothing to teach

you. I'm just older. That's it. Everything I can do, you do it better already."
"That's not true."

"You're the one with the HBO show. At what. Twenty-five?"

"You have your book."

"No one reads books anymore. They're an outdated medium. Besides, no one has time. How could they. It's the end of the world."

"I'll read your book," Nia said. "If you finish it. Will you? Do you promise?" *I feel so ashamed. I want the Uber to swallow me and I die.*

"Sure."

"You aren't mad at me, are you?"

"No. Of course not. Are you mad at me?"

"No," she said. "If we were mad at each other...I would be sad."

+

By the time we got back to the apartment, it was late, but earlier than I'd expected to be home. The apartment was empty. Rio was at what she described as a "skeeball bar" with her friends from work. Nia took the mostly unsmoked joint chilling in the ash tray on the kitchen table and lit it up, passed it to me. I took a hit, coughed. It was raining outside again. We'd missed the worst of it. *Damn. Who made a spliff?*

"So are you nervous?"

"About what?"

"About your show."

"Oh. I mean–sorry, one sec," she said, put her hand up to her mouth, began to cough. "Sorry. I fucking hate spliffs."

"Do you want tea or something? I can do lemon and honey."

"That sounds perfect, actually. Thank you."

I took another hit then got up, put the kettle on.

"Of course I'm nervous," Nia said. "How could I not be. I've never done....something like this before."

"You're gonna tear though," I said. The kettle was electric and transparent; inside of its glass, domed being, a film of bubbles formed at the water's surface and burst. Over and over again. Nia laughed.

"Going to what?"

"Never mind. Go on."

"Oh. I don't know. I mean, I know I can do it. It's just...I don't know. I'm scared of how much work it's going to be."

"Yeah."

"And of people not listening to me. Because I'm not a white boy or whatever. Or not being able to do what I actually want, and then it comes out bad, and I get judged for it."

"Is Marcus the showrunner?"

"Yeah."

"He always knows how to get the bag."

"I mean, I'm being a bitch by saying this, especially because he's been so nice to me, but...you know. He's not a writer. He's a producer. That's his whole thing."

The kettle flipped off. I cut the lemon into four identical wedges, squeezed two of them into two mugs. "I mean, I'm super grateful. It just feels random you know. Like, why me."

"I mean, you're a genius at Tik Tok. The visual genre rules, the platform's algorithm–you fucking mastered them. That's a real accomplishment. I'm being totally sincere."

"I'm good at Tik Tok now, but soon there's going to be a new app–we don't even know what it's called because it still doesn't exist. Mark Zuckerburg hasn't grown it in a petri dish yet. But when it comes out–I'll try to learn it to keep up. But it won't be the same as kids who are getting on it at sixteen, seventeen. And then one of them will come in and they'll be the ingenue. And they'll replace me."

"It won't be your fault. There's no infrastructure to have a career past your mid-thirties. That is, if you're one of the lucky ones who even makes it that far..."

"Then you can still make stuff but everyone thinks it's corny."

"You're doomed to embarrass yourself."

"Do you want more tea?" She looked down at her cup.

"Oh. Um. Only if you're making it." She passed me her cup, then picked up the grinder and weed on the table, began to roll another joint.

"In a way, it doesn't matter what I think about all this, really. Unless I become, like, stupid rich, I'll have to keep making stuff to make money until I die. So either I'll figure it out, or I'll like–invest my savings in crypto and move somewhere cheap so that I can retire by forty-five. I don't know." She ripped a piece of cardboard off the box of kleenex on the kitchen table, rolled it between her fingers until it became a cylinder, popped the filter inside the joint.

"Maybe the world won't even exist then," I said. "And neither will we. So you won't have to worry about it."

"RIP." The tick of the kettle going off. I passed the joint back to Nia and got up to make the tea.

"It's so funny you still say that."

"What."

"RIP."

"Why?"

"It''s not bad," she said. "It's just...funny. Did I tell you, you were in my dream last night. We were in this beautiful room. It was like someone had hollowed out a really big rock and let us stay inside. The windows were made of stained glass circles and it smelled really good."

"What did it smell like?"

"Like fresh rosemary and pine."

"Lyrical."

"Ha ha. I know."

"And I was there?"

"Yeah. We were there together. And some other people, too, but I didn't know who they were. We just kind of chilled. And then, one by one, people started getting up and leaving. They'd just get up and start walking through this wooden door, which was intricately carved but also seemed to be made of a single piece of wood. Very neo-feudalism. Very *Bloodborne* vibes. After a while, it was just you and me, so we got up, too. We didn't know where we were going, but we didn't know where else to go. And when we opened the door, it led into this very long tunnel, and when we got out, we were in this kind of medieval amphitheater with all the Roman architecture. Arched walls, columns, but also like ancient, falling apart."

"Like an area? Like for gladiator matches and shit?"

"Yeah. Or bull fights. When we were still working on the show, I k-holed for a bit researching them. You know, for that scene where Serena and Blair…"

"Have to fight each other to the death."

"Yeah."

"So is that what happened?" I said. "In your dream? Like straight up *Hunger Games*, *Squid Game* shit? We fought each other to the death?"

"I don't know," Nia said. "That's when I woke up."

The Very Last Ending Ends

The final *Gossip Girl* novel actually written by Cecily Von Ziegesar was *Nothing Can Keep Us Together*, published in 2005. The next five books, published from 2006-2009, were by an anonymous ghostwriter. Why didn't she write them herself? What else was she up to? r/GossipGirl reveals that von Ziegesar's ghost writer was a woman named Annabelle Vestry, who is listed as a co-author on Amazon, if not on the covers themselves.

Under a thread called "Why were the later books ghostwritten," user youreastonefox speculates that "due to their success, Cecily's publishing company ordered way more books than she'd originally intended to write for the series and she probably didn't wanna just force it so she handed the writing reigns off to Anabelle Vestry." *Gossip Girl*'s Wiki Fandom page lists Vestry as the author of a *Gossip Girl* spinoff called *The Carlyles*, but Vestry herself is a proxy. Blank.

So of course we were all surprised. When Cecily came back. Or, that's not true. All big books are franchised now. Just look at JK Rowling, eating M&Ms at the Harry Potter musical. So it was less weird that she did and more weird what she did, which was to release *Gossip Girl: Psycho Killer* in 2011, three years after the market crashed.

Unlike traditional sequels, which add to the world of the book, *Psycho Killer* redid the first *Gossip Girl* novel except with a slasher plot. "Welcome to New York City's Upper East Side," reads the first page. "Where my friends and I live and go to school and play–and sometimes kill each other."

It's good for some things to die sometimes. Otherwise, how would they end.

The fantasy of endlessness is unsurprising for Von Ziegesar on the level of content, but not of form, since her books end, promptly and schematically, with a blog post from *Gossip Girl*. "Well, I had a great time at Kiss-or-Die," reads *Psycho Killer*'s final note. "I must have lost fifteen pounds dancing–or maybe someone's chopped off my legs and I just haven't noticed. Needless to say, I'm feeling good. I mean, I survived…"

The only time I met Lauren IRL was at an academic conference in 2019. I was in my first year of graduate school. I'd interviewed them earlier that year, but didn't know if they'd recognize me. We'd only spoken over Google Docs, text, and GChat; we never saw each other's face. I sat near them–by accident or on purpose, I have no short-term memory. Once I realized, I tried to hide how much I was zoning out in case they looked at me. After the lectures ended (Lauren had delivered the keynote talk), I introduced myself, and we spoke briefly. It was fun, but they were tired, and I was stressed. We could both tell.

"Let's give Lauren time to rest," said another professor, linking arms with Lauren and steering them towards the refreshments line.

"Of course."

"We'll talk soon," they said. That was the last time we saw each other.

I can't talk to Lauren so I write to them, letters that can't be sent or received. In "The Miseducation of a French Feminist," Jules Gill-Peterson wonders if Luce Irigiray, her former teacher, "might visit me again in a dream. I'd like to see in her eyes the feeling of recognition without sameness."

In computer programming, a proxy functions as the intermediary between a client requesting a resource and the server that provides it. But proxy politics can also refer to the practice by which one person or group votes on behalf of another. As noted by the Research Center for Proxy Politics (co-founded by artist Hito Steyerl), proxies thus both denote our post-democratic age, and the IT (computers) which enable them.

Much like an issue of *Elle* or *Vogue*, *Psycho Killer* ends with a Q&A, featuring questions from readers and stans.

Questions and Answers

Why worry about college? I'm having way too much fun right now. And there are so many questions to be answered:

*Will **S** and **N** fall in love? Or will **S** grow tired of his weed smoke and cut that lonely stoner to shreds? Or is **N** already dead?*

Will ***J*** *swear off high society and fancy dresses and make friends her age? Is she our new murderous heroine? Or is she dead too?*

Will ***V*** *ever actually blow up the school?*

Will **C** *come back from the dead–or outer space?*

Will **B** *finally breakfast at Tiffany's?*

And what other secrets does **B2 (Berlant)** *have up their infinite sleeves?*

Best keep a safe distance. Unless–like me–you can't stay away.

You know you love me.

I'll outlive you.

Xoxo,
gossip girl.

Afterword

If this book had a subtitle, it would be: "The Fantasy of Unboundaried love."

I don't want to finish this book. To finish it, to give it to you, would be to cede my own loss of control. After all, what is control if not its inverse? *It was only in moments of pure and total control that he could give into himself, feel safe*. If masochism is about ceding bodily autonomy, sadism is about controlling the limits of your space. In the room where nothing can touch you, you can do whatever you want. To quote Ageha, the protagonist of Hito Steyerl's *Lovely Andrea* (2007), "Only when being roped, do I feel free."

Restraint and desire need each other in order to exist. They are, one might say, in a codependent relationship. In 2019, I reviewed the selected diaries of Lou Sullivan, which had just been collected and published for the first time. Sullivan–America's first openly gay trans man–began journaling about his life when he was a child. His diaries begin with Beatles fan fic, love letters that he could only send to himself. "Model yourself on [The Beatles] + you'll have no worries," he writes. Does he love Paul McCartney or want to become him? Does he want to die for the Beatles or does he just want to die?

In *Gossip Girl*, Dan is both a soft boy and a cop. He wants to be Serena's everything. And when she won't let him––by denying him, for instance, full access to her interior life––he can't bear it. He feels insane. It's an individualist fantasy, but, when he acts it out, it feels real.

In 2019, Kato Trieu described wanting a body that "was not personal." I miss him. I understand him more clearly these days.

–Charlie Markbreiter (January 17th, 2022)

Thank you:

River L. Ramirez (for the cover and illustrations)
Anna Aguiar Kosicki, Maz Murray and Maxi Wallenhorst (for their edits)
My mom, dad and sister (grateful)
Precious Okoyomon (4ever)

Beatrice Adler-Bolton, Webb Allen, Sam Bodrojan, April Clark, The Death Panel Discord (especially Reading Group), Patrick Durgin, Spike Einbinder, Jules Gill-Peterson, Colby Gordon, Aurelia Guo, Wim Helf, Natalie Henry, Trisha Low, Sibyl No, Rainbow and Gravity Okoyomon, Aliya Ram, Ayesha Siddiqi, Scott McKenzie, Nana Singh, The 185 Graham Cinematic Universe, Gasira Timir, Kato Trieu (RIP), Artie Vierkant, McKenzie Wark

Everyone who read/talked to/helped me with this in any way, thank you <3

Colophon

ISBN: 979-8-9856628-1-8
Library of Congress Control Number: 2022932511

Illustrations and cover art by River L. Ramirez.
Cover design by Cory Rockliff.
Interior composition by Patrick Durgin

Published in Chicago by Kenning Editions.

This book was made possible in part by the supporters of Kenning Editions, including: Nathan Austin, Stefani Barber, Mark Booth, Charles Bernstein, David Buuck, Lisa Chen, Norma Cole, John Coletti, Joel Craig, Maxe Crandall, Terry Cuddy, Maria Damon, Nicholas DeBoer, Ian Dreiblatt, Robert Fitterman, Raymond Foye, Diane Glancy, Rodney Koeneke, David Larsen in memoriam Beth Murray, Joslyn Layne, Katy Lederer, Andrew Levy, Pamela Lu, Adalaide Morris, Chris Nealon, Jena Osman, Caryl Pagel, Elizabeth Robinson, Cynthia Sailers, Susan Schultz, Cedar Sigo, Juliana Spahr, Chuck Stebelton, Suzanne Stein, Adam Talib, John Tipton, Zhengfan Yang, and Matvei Yankelevich.

Kenning Editions is a 501(c)3 non-profit corporation. Donations are tax deductible.

Kenningeditions.com

Charlie Markbreiter's writing has been published in venues such as *Bookforum*, *Art in America*, and *The New Inquiry*, where he serves as the Managing Editor. A PhD candidate at the CUNY Graduate Center, he is also a mod of the Death Panel Discord, a free school/health justice forum. He is not a *Gossip Girl* character, or that's what you think. He lives in New York. *Gossip Girl Fanfic Novella* is his first book.

Selected Backlist

Hieroglyphs of the Inverted World, by Rob Halpern

The Chilean Flag, by Elvira Hernández, translated by Alec Schumacher

The Science of Departures, by Adalber Salas Hernández, translated by Robin Myers

título / title, by Legna Rodríguez Iglesias, translated by Katherine M. Hedeen

Stage Fright: Plays from San Francisco Poets Theater, by Kevin Killian

The Grand Complication, by Devin King

Dream of Europe: Selected Seminars and Interviews: 1984-1992, by Audre Lorde, edited by Mayra Rodriguez Castro

The Compleat Purge, by Trisha Low

Ambient Parking Lot, by Pamela Lu

Tomatoes, by Nathalie Quintane, translated by Marty Hiatt

Festivals of Patience: The Verse Poems of Arthur Rimbaud, translated by Brian Kim Stefans

The Dirty Text, by Soleida Ríos, translated by Barbara Jamison and Olivia Lott

Hannah Weiner's Open House, by Hannah Weiner, edited by Patrick Durgin

Coronavirus Haiku, by Worker Writers School, edited by Mark Nowak